I0779404

JUNE FOSTER

The Novice Ranch Hand

June Foster

"I will repay you for the years the locusts have eaten." Joel 2:25a.

Acknowledgments

Thanks to Mike Foster for his information about installing and repairing fences.

Thanks to my husband for sharing his knowledge of tools and equipment.

I'd like to thank Mike Murphrey for his information about the mission fields of Peru.

Thanks to my daughter, Kelly, for sharing her experiences about living and working in Peru as a missionary.

Chapter One

Erika Ford caught her breath. She pressed her hand on her chest, fingers splayed. No matter how many times she saw the marvel of new life, the miracle never grew old.

In the pen toward the corner of the sheep barn, Sadie balanced on all fours nuzzling her newborn as the pink, wet creature eagerly nursed. As if in awe herself, the mother sheep gazed at her baby with a look Erika could only define as amazement and pride.

Erika resisted the urge to unlatch the door to the pen to get a closer look. No. Running a sheep ranch for the last five years had taught her that she shouldn't disturb mother and lamb. They needed time alone to bond.

She took a long delicious breath and allowed herself to linger a few more minutes. Finally, she backed away from the pen and then a clump and a clack sent goosebumps up her arms. She whirled around and caught her breath.

The early morning sun shined through the barn door. Someone stood inside, but the sun only outlined a silhouette. She blinked and then rubbed her eyes. "What do you want?" She felt for her handgun in her holster.

Sure, Erika owned a ranch fifteen miles from the nearest town, but she'd only encountered a few stragglers looking for a handout through the years. She kept her fingers on her gun and squinted.

The person moved to the side, no longer silhouetted against the brilliant glare. A cowboy wearing a dark-colored Stetson and a black t-shirt wandered toward her, shoulders dipping from side to side. His square jaw shifted with the movement of tightened muscles.

Erika pulled the loaded Glock from her holster. No doubt an uninvited visitor had wandered in. The news on television and the internet spoke of immigrants traveling north in droves through their Texas borders. She couldn't take chances. "I wasn't expecting a guest so if you're not off the property immediately, I'll notify the county authorities." She held the gun with both hands and motioned it toward the barn's exit. "And I can shoot this thing if I need to."

He lifted two hands, palms toward her. If she'd read the expression in his eyes correctly, uncertainty with a pinch of panic stopped him. "Look, lady. I'm not here to harm you. I'm here because Mr. Ford hired me last evening. I'm the new ranch hand."

"That's impossible. My father, brothers, and I make those decisions together." And she doubted that Dad, Austin, and Jace, after one look at this guy, would hire him. He was too good looking, with well-shaped lips and a contoured nose. But his eyes, the color of coffee with cream, hinted that he carried a burden. Surely, her father and brothers would view this as a weakness. And the Ford men didn't care for anyone who was less than capable.

She firmed her lips. "And why should I believe you?"

The guy took two steps back. "Miss Ford, I'm to shadow Mac for a few days to learn the ropes. I already met your brothers—Jace and Austin. Before Mr. Ford left for the pasture today, he asked me to muck out the horses' stable, which I finished a few minutes ago." He lowered his hands slowly and pulled soiled gloves from his pocket as if offering proof. "Then he said to check on Sadie since she'd gone into labor." He glanced toward the ewe and her lamb. "I see she's already delivered."

Heat burned Erika's cheeks, and she clenched her teeth. This only meant one thing. Her father had made an administrative decision without consulting her—again. With a shake of her head, she holstered her gun.

Erika pushed past the new ranch hand and headed toward the exit of the wooden building which housed the sheep. How many times had Dad left her out of making necessary decisions? She was as proficient as her brothers in running this ranch. She furrowed her brows.

"Wait, ma'am. Please stay for a moment. I can see we got off to a bad start. I'm Peyton Langley," he called, his voice rich and soothing.

Erika paused and turned.

Peyton raised his right hand. "I'm sorry if I upset you. I didn't get your name." His tight muscles relaxed.

Erika took a calming breath. If the man was really who he said he was, he wasn't to blame for their family conflicts. She took a few steps toward him. "I'm Erika Ford, the youngest of Terence Ford's brood."

Peyton reached toward her and then withdrew his hand as if he'd thought better of shaking hers. "Nice to meet you. I'm sure your father was planning to inform you at the family gathering tonight about hiring me. He said I was welcome to come, too."

Erika shrugged. She was as much a part of the operation of this ranch as her father and brothers. Annoyance, like a mosquito biting into her skin, burrowed into her patience, but what could she do now? The man had been hired.

She'd already told Dad she'd take care of Sadie. Why did he have to ask the new hand to do it? Though they needed another worker on the ranch, Erika hated to see this guy get caught up in a family feud.

Peyton didn't move as the Ford woman walked out of the sheep barn. She wore a holster at her waist. Her tight jeans fit her well and hinted of her womanly shape. Long hair hung in curls beneath her brown felt hat and flowed down the back of her blue shirt. No doubt, he'd met a genuine rancher.

Wait! What was he doing? He hadn't looked at another woman like that since …

He jerked his head away to watch Sadie nuzzling her newborn. The tips of Sadie's ears looked as if someone had dipped them in black ink, and the spots on her nose resembled freckles. The lamb had similar markings on its ears and nose.

Life with flocks of sheep, horse pens, and gun wielding women—nothing he'd ever experienced before. But in time, he'd make a good sheep herder—right?

He thanked God for the chance to live on this earth another day. Perhaps he could bury his past beneath the hay in the sheep barn, or under the shovels, ladder, and electric drills of the tool shed. Maybe he could hide in the hay barn or in the grassland of Texas's hill country. The farther he could get from his memories, the better off he'd be.

Peyton stepped out of the barn, pulled his cell phone from his back pocket, and checked the time. One hour until dinner at the sprawling Ford ranch house that loomed before him. He walked in the other direction toward his residence, the bunkhouse he shared with two other ranch hands. He pushed through the front door of the log cabin style building, waved at Mac on the other side of the room, and headed to the shower. A fresh change of shirt and jeans would be appropriate for meeting the family, he figured.

After his shower, he plodded across the cowhide rug in the sizeable bedroom he shared with the others and plopped down on his twin bed in one corner of the room. Not a bunk bed as he'd anticipated. Bending down, he pulled on his black leather boot with the round toe and one inch heel. Although purchasing authentic ranch shoes had proved a bit of a challenge, the salesman in the San Antonio store assured him this pair was of high quality.

He glanced at his image in the mirror atop the chest of drawers and raked a comb through his brown hair that he'd cut short. Rubbing his fingers over the stubble, he figured he better shave and then decided against it. This wasn't a job interview for a corporate position.

Besides, he'd had his fill of dress suits in sky-high office buildings, the executive washroom, and employees clawing to get ahead.

On the other side of the room, Mac, the middle-aged, seasoned wrangler, stood next to his bed and buttoned up a dark gray western-style shirt. He'd combed his brown hair, streaked with gray, over to the side. His leathery skin revealed wrinkles around his eyes and on his forehead, no doubt attesting to years of outdoor work. "So, I'll see you up at the big house? We eat with the family most nights. Mrs. Ford is an excellent cook."

"Yeah. Our boss seems to be a pleasant fellow, as well." Peyton wouldn't mention that one of the family members hadn't been quite as congenial.

"You gettin' settled in?" Mac tucked in his shirt and hung another in his small closet near his bed.

"I am, thanks. I was surprised our place was this nice inside. I pictured wall to wall bunk beds, a wood burning stove, and an outhouse."

Mac took a few steps toward Peyton. "Mr. Ford's a generous man. Our bunkhouse isn't luxurious, but it's more than adequate. Indoor plumbing and all." He slapped Peyton's shoulder. "Come on, I'll walk with you to dinner. I think Chet, the other hand, is already up there."

Peyton frowned. Meeting the entire family was daunting. But showing up for the first time accompanied by Mac seemed a lot better than going in alone.

"Hey Peyton, don't look so worried. You'll like it here, even if you are pretty green as a ranch hand."

"Green? Why do you say that?"

A wide smile crossed Mac's face. "I've been working on a ranch for twenty-five years. I can spot a rookie when I see one."

Chapter Two

In the living room as her family gathered for dinner, Erika tightened her fists and swallowed the annoyance creeping up her throat. She gaped at her brother Jace, his string tie secured under his shirt collar as if he was trying to look official and show everyone that he was second in command around here. His wife, Charlotte stood close by.

"I found two ewes and one lamb on the north pasture this morning. Some animal had a tasty meal, I'm afraid." He grimaced and combed his hand through his dark blond hair.

Erika's other brother, Austin, bit his lip, his blue eyes blazing. "Did you see evidence of the culprit?"

"The predator, you mean?" Jace stood, legs in a wide stance, and crossed his arms over his chest. "Yes. Coyote scat and tracks."

Erika frowned. She'd ignore her brother's display of superiority. No matter what, something had to be done. "We need to go on coyote patrol. Shoot every last one of them." Her voice raised in pitch. "I volunteer to be first." She shifted her gaze from Jace to the two people entering the house through the front door.

Mac held one of the double doors for the new ranch

hand, and the two walked through the entrance and past the river rock fireplace that extended across one wall in the living room.

She stared at the handsome guy wearing a royal blue shirt, jeans, and shiny boots that looked like they came straight out of a box.

Dad glanced up from the conversation with the family and smiled at the new hand. "Oh, hello, Peyton. I don't believe you've met my daughter, Erika."

Peyton walked up beside Dad and nodded at Erika. "Actually, we met earlier today."

Dad raised his brows. "Earlier today?"

"Yes, in the sheep barn, Dad. He informed me he was the new hand." She eyed her father, wondering if he caught the significance of her words. She wouldn't mention how she pulled a gun on him.

Did she imagine the fine line of droplets across Peyton's forehead? "I'm sorry we had a misunderstanding earlier." She held out her hand. "Truce?"

Dad frowned. "Truce? What happened."

"Oh, nothing, Dad. Everything's okay now."

Peyton's lips relaxed into a smile, and he shook her hand. "Truce. I apologize for frightening you."

How could his face ever frighten her? "No worries." She stared into his eyes a moment too long.

Mac tapped Peyton's arm. "See you later, buddy. I'm heading to the dining room."

"Yeah. Later." Peyton glanced at Charlotte next to Jace.

Dad looked up. "Oh, and this is my daughter-in-law Charlotte, Jace's wife."

Peyton nodded at Charlotte. "A pleasure, ma'am."

A gentleman, Erika assumed. And quite a charmer. Well, she wouldn't fall for that appeal.

Charlotte pushed her dark rimmed glasses up on the bridge of her nose and held out her well-rounded hand. "Same here." With a thin smile, she turned back to Jace. If she noticed the new guy's good looks, it didn't show.

Dad thrust out his chest. "And then there's my oldest son Tim. He's a doctor at Lubbock General." Dad looked at Mom with his usual affectionate gaze. No doubt, after all these years, they were still in love—and proud of their oldest child. "And this is my wife of almost forty years."

"Nice to meet you, ma'am." As with Charlotte, Peyton shook her hand.

Dad slipped his arm around Mom. "About half the time, she does the cooking with Charlotte's help. Other times, we hire a chef. My lovely wife deserves a break sometimes." Dad kissed her cheek.

Erika wrinkled her nose. No doubt Dad appreciated Mom's hard work. Too bad he didn't see his own daughter's efforts around the ranch in the same way. Of course, Mom lived up to his expectations—staying busy in the home. Erika, on the other hand, pursued jobs—shoeing horses, rounding up sheep in the pasture, and repairing fence lines.

Erika jerked her attention to Peyton again—a distraction from the rising irritation.

Peyton glanced toward the kitchen and sniffed a couple of times. "Something smells wonderful."

Mom, her graying hair up in a bun, looked at Dad with what Erika would describe as an adoring smile. "I love to feed hungry men. Tonight, we're having a typical Texas feast: brisket, coleslaw, slow-cooked pinto beans with salt pork and spices, potato salad, bolillos, and coconut cream pie.

Delight emerged on Peyton's face, and he rubbed his stomach. "Sounds delicious."

Not only was Peyton easy on the eyes, he was polite, unlike other hands who'd worked on the ranch. Had he experienced the pressures of the industry—long hours in the sun or rain, the ability to perform hard labor, and possession of riding skills? From the look of his light skin tone and lack of sun spots, he didn't work outside much. Maybe he was new to the business.

"Shall we head into the dining room?" Dad rested his fingers at Mom's waist.

The crowd moseyed into the room with the hardwood oak table that filled most of the space along with the pale green, fabric-covered chairs. The family portrait on the back wall displaying Grandma and Grandpa Ford and Erika's great grandparents who'd founded the ranch made her heart pound with pride.

Dad pointed to the second table. "Peyton, the hands generally sit there."

As Erika took her seat at the family table, she stole another peek at Peyton.

He closed his eyes and bowed his head even before her father spoke the blessing.

Dad folded his hands. "Let's thank God for our food."

Peyton wore a warm smile—like he felt comfortable in God's presence. Praying was likely something he ordinarily did—like Erika's grandmother who'd always said praying to God would bring peace to her heart.

But Erika needed to know more about the new

hand. What kind of work had he done before coming here, and why had he taken the ranch hand's job? Maybe Dad could tell her more about the new employee he'd hired.

Peyton peeked at the big table to make sure the Fords had begun to eat before he tried a bite. In the center of the family table, a vase on a white tablecloth held a large arrangement of zinnias and roses. Guess the family went all out for their evening meals.

Mac glanced toward the young kid sitting across from them. "Peyton, this is Chet, the other ranch hand."

Peyton nodded. "Glad to meet you, Chet."

Chet nodded and stuffed a huge bite of beans in his mouth.

Peyton's stomach gave a loud growl, and he devoured a huge bite of the tasty brisket likely cooked over post oak wood. He was hungrier than he thought. No doubt, his appetite would increase out here on the ranch. Not like six months ago … when food tasted like cardboard.

Chet munched a bite of potato salad and swallowed. His shoulders slumped, as if he was thinking about an escape plan when dinner was over. Though the skinny kid couldn't be more than seventeen or eighteen, Peyton figured he'd faced difficulty at one point in his short years on earth.

Peyton made a mental note to ask Mac more about the boy. Where was his family? Why wasn't he in school?

Another bite of brisket and Peyton dared a glance at the family table.

Erika looked toward him, and their eyes locked. Before he could blink, she turned away to her dinner partner—her mother.

When he focused on his plate, another vision intruded upon his mind—Sandra with her dark hair and blue eyes. Her joyful outlook had carried her through every day. She believed each moment to be a gift from God.

Erika was nothing like her.

Peyton gripped his fingers into a tight ball under the table. He had to stop thinking like this. His appetite fled, and he wanted to give himself a mental kick in the pants. He hadn't come to the ranch to dredge up old memories.

"Hey, pal. You ain't eatin' much." Mac stabbed a piece of brisket. "Lost your appetite?"

"No, taking a breather." No one could know about his past. They'd only try to console him, believing they were helpful. He turned to Mac with a heavy weight pressing on his stomach. "I'm saving up for that coconut cream pie."

"Good deal." Mac smiled past a bite of pinto beans.

Peyton sipped his tea. "So, tell me about tomorrow. What can I expect?" And would he be able to perform his ranch hand duties without looking like an inept fool?

Erika pushed through the wide glass doors and

stepped out onto the covered patio. The chunky wooden furniture surrounding the outdoor fireplace tempted her to sit and soak in the stunning view of the hills covered with low lying brush and redbud trees.

No. She had to talk to Dad who'd strolled outside only moments ago.

Her father stood at the edge of the cedar deck, arms crossed, and probably in deep thought.

She touched his shoulder. "Can we talk a moment?"

He glanced around. "Erika? Sure, anytime. What's up?"

He might say he was available to talk, but if she brought up a subject he didn't want to discuss, he'd suddenly have something important to take care of.

Erika blew out a breath of air. Sometimes she didn't understand her father. If he was so open to accommodating her, then why hadn't he included her in ranch decisions? Like yesterday when he hired Peyton Langley.

Erika longed to stroll through the grass toward the North Pasture and then the rolling hills—to get a better view of the pink and purple clouds floating close to the horizon. But she couldn't put off confronting her father. "The sunset's beautiful tonight."

Dad ran a hand through his graying hair. "The sunset? Oh, yes, yes. What's on your mind, Erika?"

She had her father's attention. She'd best speak up. "The new hire, Peyton Langley. Why didn't you tell me before you hired him? I thought you, me, Jace, and Austin were a team, that we'd make administrative decisions together."

Dad grasped her hand and patted her fingers, giving her a furtive smile.

If she didn't know better, she'd believe he treated her like a helpless child. Had he merely patronized her? A coyote's early evening yip and then howl launched a chill down her spine.

"You'll recall at the last family meeting, I mentioned that I needed to hire another worker." He glanced toward the house and back, as if this conversation made him uncomfortable.

She folded her arms over her chest and stood taller. "Yes, but we didn't discuss who or when."

Dad gave her hand another pat. "I'm sorry, honey. I've been busy looking into marketing options for our sheep's wool." As if he figured she wouldn't understand, he glanced at his watch and then toward the house again. That important *something* he needed to take care of.

Annoyance rolled around in her chest. "Maybe you have, but Peyton told me he'd already met Jace and Austin. You must've informed them." She took a breath as the volume of her voice threatened to rise.

"I caught up with them in the sheep barn yesterday morning and mentioned it." Dad lifted his brows. "So, you're getting acquainted with Peyton?"

She sipped in a breath. She'd experienced this reaction before, deflecting the attention from the actual subject. But she couldn't give her father a negative impression of Peyton. "He came into the barn to check on Sadie at the same time I was there. After I pulled a gun on him, he explained how he'd met Jace and Austin."

"What?" Dad's eyes widened.

"What was I to expect?" She tightened her fists. Did Dad think she should allow a complete stranger to mosey into the barn while she was there alone? She shook her head. "No problem. He's hired now." If he didn't pick up on the sarcasm in her voice, she'd be surprised.

She turned back to the house but then faced Dad again. "If I might ask, what do you know about this guy?" Maybe her father had discovered something that would clue her into Peyton's past.

"The new hand? He answered my ad in *Ranch Life Today*. Said he was from Dallas and had a degree in business administration with a minor in psychology. When I met with him, he showed me his driver's license and a copy of his college diploma."

"Why in the world would he want to work on a ranch with that background?" Erika rolled her eyes. "Sounds like he might be overqualified."

"Peyton mentioned he was ready for a change. Though he didn't have experience on a ranch, said he grew up on the back of a horse after he took riding lessons."

"So, you up and hired him." Erika bit her tongue. She had to curtail the disappointment her father didn't include her in ranch business.

Dad stared at her as if attempting to figure out where she was heading with all this. "I hired him because he's educated and seems to be a man with character. He told me attending church is important to him."

"Attends church?" Erika shook her head. "That qualifies him to work on a ranch?"

Her father firmed his lips. "Erika. I'm not sure I like your attitude. The man also showed me a letter of recommendation from the president of James, Tucker, and Elliot of Dallas, a major marketing firm." Dad pinned her with his stare. "The guy is determined to start a new life. He can learn how to do his job."

"Don't you think it's a little dubious that someone with all those qualifications would want to work as a ranch hand?"

"Absolutely not. Many people love working in the out-of-doors with herds of sheep or cattle. Your brothers, for example. I see nothing suspicious about Peyton Langley."

She took a long breath in an attempt to settle her nerves. "Did he say what happened that he needed to go in a different direction?"

"No. He only said he'd spent time outside the United States after working in a corporate job in Dallas, and now he planned to settle in Texas."

"Okay." Taking a deep breath, she stood on tiptoe and gave Dad's cheek a kiss. "I'm sorry I got a little irritated. See you in the morning." She didn't want him to believe she was okay with leaving her out of decisions, but at the same time, she didn't want to go to bed angry.

Erika climbed the stairs to her bedroom on the second floor. She stared out the wide window toward the north. The clouds had turned to a darker orange and yellow.

Below Dad stood looking toward the sunset, his hands in a prayer position.

She had to face the truth. Though her father loved her, his idea of her job description differed from hers. She bit her lip until it hurt. One day Dad would retire, and only last week Jace had mentioned that he wanted to purchase his own ranch in a few years. Who would run the Ford ranch then? Austin? Not alone. And Tim wasn't about to leave his medical practice. Only one thing to do. Strongly communicate to her father that she'd keep the ranch going someday after he retired, and she needed the experience now.

Erika slipped on her pajamas and strolled to the cabinet near the window. She picked up the envelope laying on top marked with her bank's return address. The information inside sent a sense of accomplishment, and then the year she'd turned sixteen surfaced in her memory.

At her grandfather's suggestion, she'd opened a savings account. Later, she'd transferred the money to mutual funds, and she'd seen her balance grow.

"One of these days you'll need the capital," Grandpa had assured her.

So, she'd developed a plan. When the primary load of the ranch was hers, she'd benefit from the resource. But why did she get the idea that Dad didn't want her to eventually run the ranch? What was he not telling her?

Chapter Three

Peyton drained his coffee mug, king-sized like everything else in Texas and pushed away from the table laden with bacon, fried eggs, and hot biscuits with butter and strawberry jam. Couldn't ask for anything tastier than Mrs. Ford and Charlotte's cooking. Well, except for his mom's ability in the kitchen.

Someone slapped his back. "The boss said it'll be a couple more days until we start shearing."

Peyton turned to Mac behind him.

Mac slipped his thumbs under his suspenders. "I happen to be one of the best sheep shearers in our state so you'll be well trained." His loud guffaw said he enjoyed his joke.

Peyton chuckled. "Since you know I'm a rookie, you won't be surprised that you have your work cut out for you." He followed Mac from the dining room, through the large living room and out the front door.

"Aw, you'll do fine." Mac paused on the wraparound front porch. "What brought you to the Ford ranch?"

He'd wanted to avoid the question. He wasn't one to lie, but he could be vague with the truth. "I was ready for a change."

Rain pinged a steady beat on the metal roof overhead and puddled on the lush, green lawn.

"Got rain gear, man?" Mac glanced at the dark sky. "Rainy season usually doesn't start for another month, but I guess we forgot to tell Mother Nature."

"No, I need to go into town for a jacket."

"No problem. But for now, there're plenty of rain slickers in the horse stable. The boss said he wants you to ride along with Erika to the west pasture and check on fence lines today. I'm heading to the bunkhouse for my poncho. See you at lunch." Mac jogged toward their quarters, pulling his hat farther down on his head.

A little rain never hurt anyone. Peyton started out in a slow trot, sweeping drops of moisture from his eyes. The white wooden building which housed the horses lay ahead. He pushed through the wide door leading to the interior and glanced around at the separate enclosures lining each wall divided by a concrete floor. The fresh aroma of hay, leather, tack, and cedar shavings transported him back to his riding lessons as a teen.

Toward the end of the stable, Erika brushed an appaloosa's spotted coat. She glanced up. "I'm riding Paint today. You want to take Jack?" She pointed to the Mustang in the next stall.

"Sure. As long as you train me how to check fences." He'd said he wanted a change. Well, he'd gotten one.

"Will do." She gathered her bridle, reins, and bit and hoisted her saddle atop Paint. "You can use the one over there." Erika pointed to the tack room at the front of the barn.

Peyton hoisted Jack's saddle on his back and

cinched the leather straps. He put on his rain gear and swung his leg over the horse.

"Follow me." Erika donned a rainslicker and climbed atop Paint. She nudged him out on the paved road in front of the big house and turned east onto a dirt-covered road—now soaked with mud.

After fifteen minutes, the rain gradually slacked, and Peyton flipped the hood of his raincoat onto his back.

Erika, obviously a natural on top of a horse, circled around to him and nodded toward the east. "The wire and rail fence line Dad had installed about fifteen years ago begins over there." The land rose and dipped, the horse hooves throwing slush up with every step. "We'll inspect about three miles today. Summer storms get fierce around here. Keep an eye out for trees that have fallen over the wire."

Peyton inhaled a long breath of wet cedar and mesquite trees. Grassy hills covered in blue and purple lupines dissolved into the stony hills in the distance living up to the area's name—The Texas Hill Country. "The bluebonnets are pretty this time of year."

Erika looked up and nodded. "I'm glad they're in the distance. We need to keep a careful eye out for them in the pastures. They're deadly to the sheep."

He hadn't known that fact about lupine. Must've been a pretty intense job—keeping them out of the sheep's pastures. Birds or the wind could easily spread the seed. Peyton chuckled under his breath. He'd never look at the beautiful lupines the same again.

"Be sure to watch for tears in the wire or any of the wooden posts that appear rotten or wobbly." She trotted ahead of him.

"You got it," he shouted. Peyton poked Jack's side with a gentle kick and caught up with his guide. *Would now be a bad time for casual conversation?* He searched for the courage to ask about her life. "How long have you worked for your father?"

She lifted her Stetson, brushed a strand of her long blonde hair with her fingers, and set the hat in place again. "During high school, I worked after school and on the weekends. Since I graduated from college, I work full time."

"You must be pretty good with a gun as well." He couldn't resist the urge to tease. "I got one question. Yesterday when you pulled that pistol on me, did you plan to shoot?"

Erika flashed a smile. "You bet. I've been taught never to pull my gun unless I'm ready to use it."

Erika pulled Paint's reins, slowing him to a walk. "We can circle around now and head back to the ranch. Dad will be happy to know part of the fence is secure. We'll probably ride the rest after lunch."

Peyton guided his horse beside her, his rain gear tucked away inside his saddlebag, a grin on his lips. "I think I'm going to like ranch life."

"You got a lot more to learn." Like what to do when he repaired one of those fences. "Let's go back by way of the old cattle trail." She glanced in the direction of the ranch.

Erika tucked her raingear behind her saddle and took in an easy breath. The clouds parted, allowing a peek of light blue sky. She loved ranch life out under the big sky or riding the pastures after a rain.

Ahead, the grass coverage greened as they neared the creek. Sunlight glistened and danced on the water which gurgled over small stones and pebbles. She turned to Peyton as he trotted up on his horse. "That's Coyote Creek. It originates from a spring north of here and joins a tributary to the south."

Peyton steered Jack closer to the body of water, and Erika followed.

As she neared the mesquite tree next to the stream, she squinted. A lump of something lay about three feet from the edge of the creek. "Wait. What's that?" She clicked her heels against her horse to catch up with Peyton and then grasped her throat. She hopped down from the saddle, looped the reins on a branch, and took a few hesitant steps closer to the object, hoping it wasn't what she feared.

Peyton dismounted and walked up behind her. "I'm afraid it's a sheep."

In ranching, they lost animals to a variety of circumstances. But like this —

Erika stopped a few feet from the yearling, bloodied from a predator who'd attacked and devoured a meal. She shook her head as her stomach lurched. This part of ranching weakened her.

Though Erika cringed at the scene before her, she sensed Peyton's nearness at her side and couldn't ignore his warmth. "Looks like the work of a coyote." She bit her lip, trying to steady her voice. "You might know. The stream is called Coyote Creek."

Peyton moved closer to the carcass. "What happens now? Do we leave it here?"

"Yes." She pulled out her cell phone. "I'll ask Austin to come for it in the ATV and take the remains to the landfill in the west pasture."

Once she'd buried a young lamb on site, and it had taken all the composure she had. Dad had reprimanded her. She pinched her lips tight. At least she hadn't left it there, but then Dad always seemed hard to please.

Peyton looked at her with an understanding nod.

As though hypnotized, she couldn't pull her attention from his gaze. Something inside softened. Try as she may to keep it there, she let go of a firmly held façade she allowed no one else to see. Peyton had sensed her dread of finding animals lost to predators yet didn't mock her. Finally, his kind eyes released hers.

She mounted Paint again. "We'll follow the trail to the left back to the ranch." The sound of Jack's hooves trotting along behind assured her that Peyton followed. If she thought about the dead lamb too long, she'd have to admit how sad she became when they lost one of the flock—and she hoped Peyton hadn't figured it out.

After fifteen minutes, they tied their horses to the post in front of the main house. Erika patted Peyton's shoulder. "Great job, today. Mac will be happy to learn you're picking up ranching skills quickly."

Once again, his coffee and cream eyes seized her breath. Too quickly, he glanced away. "Thanks. Got a good trainer today."

Had the handsome cowboy sensed the connection between them and her vulnerability out there by Coyote Creek? Hopefully, he hadn't felt the powerful attraction that drew her to him. Not only physically, but there was something else she couldn't define.

The evening breeze cooled Peyton's cheeks as he left the Ford residence and headed toward the bunkhouse. Meatloaf, mashed potatoes, green beans. One thing about ranch life, the food was plentiful and delicious. And Erika's family were accommodating folks.

Erika.

Something had stirred in her today when they came across the dead lamb. He witnessed a soft side he hadn't seen before.

He paused at the door to the log building. Maybe he'd check on the ewes and their lambs tonight. He snickered. He had to see if his wooly buddies were doing okay.

Wooden dividers lined the walls where ewes were housed with their lambs that arrived almost daily these days. He stopped at the first pen. A newborn sheep standing on wobbly legs wiggled his pink ears as he greedily nursed with more vigor than the ranch hands eating their dinner. He propped his boot on the horizontal wooden divider and closed his eyes. The sound of mother sheep bleating and baaing to their young reminded him again that he stood in a sheep barn—a significant change from last year.

He took several long breaths hoping to quell the thought rising in his heart. The truth refused to be held captive any longer. He opened his mouth, with only the lambs and ewes as his audience. "The loss was too much, Sandra—and our unborn child. I know it's time, but I'm not ready." He opened his eyes as if the answer would appear on the barn wall. "Where do I go from here?"

Realization dawned inside bringing a ray of understanding. His job here at the ranch included shepherding Mr. Ford's sheep. He was to protect them from thieves and predators, as God did for His people.

Something brushed the back of his leg, and he reached toward his jeans. His fingers met a ball of fur, and he jumped to the side, his eyes wide open. Was it a fox who'd wandered into the barn—or a coyote?

A black and white border collie, his eyes bright and his tongue lolling from his mouth as if smiling wagged his tail. He nudged Peyton's hand, as if asking for another pat.

"Hey, where did you come from?" He stroked the soft fur on top of the animal's head, soothing Peyton's anxious thoughts.

"Sam, are you giving our new ranch hand a hard time?" Erika headed toward him from the barndoor. "Don't worry." She grinned at Peyton. "This guy's a member of the family, and he works here."

Peyton blew out a short breath. "For a minute there … "

"I saw you walk into the barn. I figured you were checking on the sheep, and I wanted to thank you for helping me with the slain lamb." She reached to pet Sam. "I don't like to share this with everyone, but somehow I feel I can trust you."

Peyton eyed her. "Of course."

"It's hard for me seeing a dead sheep. Always has been—although I don't admit it to Dad and my brothers."

She'd confessed a personal challenge to him, which

surprised him. Peyton grinned at Erika. "Don't worry. I'm not one for passing on information." He stroked Sam's warm fur again and grasped the dog's paw for a shake. "I'm glad to meet another person in the Ford family."

Peyton returned to the bunkhouse and sank down into one of the lawn chairs sitting in front. The Ford family. Erika, her father and brothers, even Sam, not much different than his. Even Mrs. Ford's cooking equaled his mom's.

Mom.

How long had it been seen he'd seen her? Too long. Peyton dialed his dad's phone. Maybe they'd be at home for a chat. After two rings, Dad answered.

"Hey, Son. How's it going? Your mom and I were just talking about you. Here, let me put you on video call."

"Hey, Peyton." Mom's sweet face appeared on the screen. Her short, dark hair framed bright eyes and smiling lips. "I've missed my oldest son."

"Mom, I'm your only son."

Her pleasant laugh reminded him of the time when he'd first learned to ride his bike, and she'd said how proud she was of him. "How are things on that sheep ranch?"

"I'm learning a lot. It's nice to have my mind on something different."

"Son, I pray for you and your loss every day. I pray that the Lord will fill your life with healing and blessings."

Peyton could always depend on Mom to understand the things of his heart. "I'm gonna make it. The open pastures and farm animals are helping to mend that which was broken in my life."

"Hey, Son." Dad's smiling face appeared on the phone's screen. "When you think you're coming home for a visit?"

"Not sure right now, but I hope at least before next Christmas."

The screen switched to Mom's image as Dad kiss her cheek, and she giggled. "Well, when you do, I'll have your favorite meal waiting for you. Fried chicken, mashed potatoes, and lemon pie."

He had to admit, his mom's was the best. He waved at his parents. "I love you both. See you soon."

Until he clicked off the call, Peyton didn't realize how much he missed his family. His mother who loved him unconditionally and his dad who would sacrifice anything to help Peyton. Could he possibly leave for a visit within the next months?

Chapter Four

Peyton wadded his napkin and set it next to his empty plate which only moments ago held scrambled eggs, waffles, and crispy bacon. He rose from his chair and passed the breakfast buffet set up near the kitchen. He chuckled under his breath. If he didn't know better, he'd believe he was a guest at an elegant B & B.

But the bleating of sheep as he walked out the front door of the stately home and onto the wide sidewalk reminded him, he was here to do a job. Which was fine with him. How could he enjoy a leisurely vacation—without Sandra?

Mac ambled from the outside entrance to Mr. Ford's office and approached Peyton. "Boss says you and Chet are mucking out the sheep barn this morning. Don't forget to look under the feeders where hay can fall out and check the small nooks around the area. Mr. Ford likes a clean space for his flock."

"Sure thing, Mac. Couldn't be too much different than cleaning a horse stall. Done that a bunch of times." Peyton picked up his pace to catch up with Chet leaving the bunkhouse. "I hear we're on sheep pen duty today. Where do you suggest we start?"

Chet turned to glance in Peyton' direction, his brown hair protruding from his hat and curling around his ears. A sprinkle of freckles dotted his nose and cheeks, giving him a boyish look. "I figured you were going to tell me how it's done."

Peyton snickered. "I'm not as skilled as you may think." Best not to reveal to the kid this was his first experience at ranching. But he wanted to get him talking, if possible.

"I done it a couple of times before—the first job Mr. Ford gave me after I come to work here." He started out for the barn.

Peyton paused a moment next to the outer wooden wall of the sheep barn. "So, how long ya been here, buddy?"

Chet's hands hung lifeless and loose beside him. His slouched shoulders gave the impression he needed stability and direction—same as Peyton a year ago.

"Oh, jest a couple of months." He coughed and then shut his mouth. Like Peyton had figured, Chet wasn't much of a talker.

"I'm interested. How did you wind up on a sheep ranch?" Peyton persisted yet he was glad no one had asked him the same question.

"Things jest turned out like that." Chet studied his skinned-up boots and scratched the back of his neck. "Guess we better get started."

Peyton followed the teen into the sheep barn. Though he wanted to know much more about him, he'd let it rest for now. The longing in the young man's face stirred a sense of compassion. If Peyton wasn't wrong, Chet had suffered as Peyton had. Was there any way he could help?

Erika stuffed the two sack lunches into her saddle bag and loosened the red and white bandana around her neck. The balmy weather of late March didn't surprise her, and hotter days would be here soon.

Peyton ambled toward her from the horse barn, Jack trotting behind. "Sheep barn's done, and it's not even time for lunch yet." His broad smile lit his face.

A glance at the cowboy's long strides and straight hips flooded her with interest in this mysterious man. "Yep. Dad's glad to have you working on the Ford ranch."

He tightened the saddle on Jack's back and climbed on. "Your father said he wants us to round up the dry ewes and some rams in the north pasture today."

"Yeah, and I've got a couple of lunches since we'll miss the noon meal." Erika stepped onto the stirrup and swung her leg over Paint.

Peyton glanced toward the ranch's sheep dog. "Sam coming, I presume?"

"We couldn't bring those sheep in without him." She whistled for Sam and nudged Paint's side.

Sam raced toward Erika from the edge of the barn. "Jace and Austin took this herd out about two weeks ago to help clear the pasture. The sheep always do a good job."

Peyton gave Jack a couple of pats under his long mane. "Tell me about how Sam works."

He either faked being a novice, or he was truly inexperience on a sheep ranch. "Sam drives the flock forward in the direction we want them to go." Again, the desire to know more about this city guy-turned-cowboy prompted her curiosity. What kind of job did he have before he came to the ranch? What was his life like? "Generally, one of us rides in front and the other in back. Sheep have a strong instinct to follow the one in front of them, so if we can guide the first animal forward, we've got it made."

Peyton smiled. "Can I ride in the back my first time?" His awkward snicker convinced her—he'd never spent time rounding up sheep on a ranch before.

"You may not have much experience, but Dad always looks for hands that want to learn. He wants employees who're willing to work hard. I believe that describes you."

Peyton peered at her a moment and then jiggled the reins to command the horse to trot faster.

She winced. Maybe she'd embarrassed the guy with her flattery though she'd only spoken the truth.

The greening grass and the buzzing of locusts and katydids signaled spring had arrived—Erika's favorite season. Twenty minutes later, she hopped off Paint and unlatched the gate to the field in the north pasture. "Come on through, and we can have lunch before we round up the sheep." She beckoned Peyton with a crook of her hand and tied Paint to the redbud tree. "Please close the gate after you and Jack." She grinned. "We don't want the sheep to escape."

"I see how fencing plays an important part on a sheep ranch." Peyton called for Jack to come through the gate and tied him to a tree near Paint.

Erika retrieved the lunches from her saddlebag and headed toward the cluster of oak trees growing toward the east. "As a kid, I always loved to bring a picnic lunch here and pretend I was the ranch hand in charge. I imagined we were getting ready to round up the sheep and bring them back to the ranch to be sheered. The flock dotted the landscape all around, and I wasn't sure if we could manage the whole bunch. But of course, in my daydream, the sheep obediently turned toward the barn before a threatening rainstorm."

"So, you always wanted to be the boss?" Peyton leaned against the oak's trunk.

"Uh, huh. While some girls played with dolls, I hung out with ranch animals."

Peyton sipped a swig of water. "Do the flocks frequently remain in the pasture overnight?"

"Good question. We don't always bring them back to the barn, especially in the summer when we need the pasture cleared of grass."

"What about the hands? Do they ever stay overnight with them?"

"I don't think you'll have to worry about camping out too frequently. We have a small flock and smaller pastures, for example, than ranches in South America. They're easier to monitor here at the Ford ranch." She pointed toward the hills. "See that creature over there?"

Peyton laughed. "Yeah, a donkey."

"That's Fred. Donkeys are strong guard animals with excellent hearing. Fred's loud bray discourages most predators. Of course, that's not always the case."

"True."

When Sam moseyed toward Peyton as if looking for a treat, Peyton raised his palms in the air. "Sorry, buddy. You better see Erika for a snack."

Erika laughed and passed Sam a dog biscuit from a

plastic bag. "Only one. You've got your work to do first."

"Does that mean I don't get to eat until I round up a bunch of sheep first?" He eyed the sandwiches, deviled eggs, and chocolate cookies.

Though he seemed quiet and mysterious, Peyton displayed a sense of humor which she liked. She chuckled and handed him a plate filled with the lunch Charlotte had prepared. "Okay, so you're special. But I warn you. Sam will be jealous. He could be looking for a handout. We don't allow him to beg."

"No worries. Not gonna share with Sam." Peyton held the plate in his lap and bit off a mouthful of the chicken salad sandwich.

Erika passed Peyton a bottle of water and took a swig of hers. A warm breeze lifted her hair beneath her Stetson. She finally dared the question she'd wanted to ask since the first day she saw him. "I don't know too much about you. I understand you have a business background. If I may ask, why did you decide to work on a sheep ranch? Wasn't that a radical change?"

Peyton gazed upward as if studying a flock of birds.

Erika glanced at the cloudless sky. No birds flew at the moment. She turned her gaze toward him again and fixed her focus on his face.

"You see, I came to a… er… point in my life—"

Sam raced between them, upsetting Erika's water bottle she'd secured on the grass between two rocks.

She righted the bottle and yelled. "Sam, what are you doing?"

"See that rabbit over there?" Peyton pointed to her left and grinned.

Sam came within a few feet of the animal.

Erika couldn't have her working dog getting distracted by a creature out in the ranch's pasture. "Come, Sam." Erika hollered at him, her opportunity to talk to Peyton about his past gone for now.

Sam scampered back, his tail between his legs.

Peyton chomped on a deviled egg and swallowed. "I've been meaning to ask. What's Chet's story."

"I don't know a lot. Dad said he came from San Antonio and that he had problems in his home. Said he was better off here. My father's going to see about helping him get his GED soon." She lifted her hands. "That's about all I know."

Dad hadn't revealed much about Chet but then he said he didn't know anything about Peyton either. No doubt her father told the truth about his newest employee. If her guess was correct, the man had walked away from a disturbing past and didn't want to share his life with anyone. She couldn't let go of the desire to know. What kind of secret did the new ranch worker hold deep within his heart?

Chapter Five

Erika opened her eyes to the sound of a gentle *flap flap*. The light breeze fluttered her curtains through the opened window. Sunlight streamed in from the east.

She flung back her bedspread, the color of the hills in the spring time. The gray and white throw rug cushioned her feet from the cold, hardwood floor. What time was it? Barefoot, she maneuvered to the bathroom.

Next time, she wouldn't stay awake half the night thinking about the new ranch hand. What good did that do? He obviously didn't want her or anyone else to discover the kind of life he'd known before. Had Peyton committed some terrible crime like robbery or embezzlement—or was he in hiding? Or perhaps he'd run away from a difficult marriage.

Erika glanced in the bathroom mirror. A strand of long, tangled hair fell in her face, and she reached for her hairbrush. She stared at the image looking back at her. Her round cheeks and full lips reminded her she was her mother's child. But that's where the similarities ended. She loved her mom but never wanted to live her life working around the house all the time.

Since Dad asked them to remain on the clock a few hours on Saturday morning, she'd better get dressed. A long-sleeved turquoise shirt and her light denim jeans would do. She swept her hair up in a pony tail and barreled down the stairs. The aroma of earthy, rich coffee called to her.

Charlotte, a sturdy cotton apron tied around her ample hips, looked up from chopping onions. " You missed breakfast." She turned to her cutting board again.

The sarcastic note in Charlotte's tone was hard to miss. "I know. I'm not hungry anyway. Just need a cup of coffee."

Charlotte nodded toward the Keurig coffee maker on the counter. "I already unplugged the coffee urn I use for the breakfast folks, but you can make a cup in the other pot if you can figure out how to operate it."

"Charlotte. I'm not that inept in the kitchen." Her sister-in-law's sarcasm wouldn't stand in the way of a cup of coffee. What was the woman's problem anyway? She always seemed uncomfortable around Erika. As if Erika had done something terrible, or as if Charlotte disapproved of her.

Erika stuck a French vanilla pod in the maker, brewed a cup, and added half and half.

"Jace would have a cow if I slept this late." Charlotte filled a bowl with diced tomatoes.

The hot, rich-flavored coffee soothed the sound of Charlotte's impertinent tone. Since they were alone at the moment, maybe Erika could chat with Charlotte. Perhaps if Erika knew Jace's wife better …   "So, what're you making for lunch today?" She sat at the round kitchen table and sipped the earthy, coffee, brewed to perfection.

Charlotte added the tomatoes to a pot on the stove.

"Spaghetti sauce." She lifted her chin, no smile on her face. "You should really take time to learn your way around the kitchen." Her brittle voice hinted of distrust—certainly not of friendship.

Erika cleared her throat. "Mom promised to teach me how to cook one of these days, but right now my job keeps me busy. Dad needs help with the everyday duties around the ranch."

"Rounding up sheep? Getting animal waste all over yourself when mucking out a barn? I can't imagine how you'd want to do that. I prefer to work in the house and provide nutritious meals."

Heat flushed through Erika. If she allowed herself, she'd tell Charlotte that if she got out of the house more often, maybe she would be a little happier and less prone to being overweight. Erika bit her lip and rose from the table, critical words begging to be said. She pressed her lips together, placed her cup in the sink, and walked out of the kitchen, her boots clicking on the hardwood floor.

"Check the animals to make sure there're no signs of illness or injury," the boss man told Peyton. "Then you're off at noon. Tomorrow, if you'd like to go, I'll take the van into town. Most Sundays we attend church."

Peyton smiled as he headed toward the sheep barn. Some of the best news he'd heard in a while. He'd have the privilege of going to church.

He scratched his head. How long had it been? Four

or five months since he'd stepped into a church. After his life had fallen apart, he hadn't attended. Not that he didn't love God, but the thought of facing all those happy people—happy couples felt daunting.

Erika marched from the house and headed toward the horse stable like an emergency demanded her attention. Hands in tight balls, she disappeared inside the barn.

Whatever bothered her was none of his business. Though he wanted to ask if she planned to go into town tomorrow, he wouldn't now.

Chet strolled toward him from the bunkhouse. "Morning, Peyton."

"I hear Mr. Ford is taking the van into town tomorrow—to church. You going?"

Chet stuffed his hands in his pocket. "Aww, I donno. Church never done nothing much for me. You?" He walked alongside Peyton toward the sheep barn.

Since the boy asked, Peyton would answer. He paused at the door, the sound of baaing and the earthy smell of dust, dirt, and grain evident. "Yes, I sure am. I've been going to church since I was a kid younger than you."

"Some people like you got it good. You probably had a nice family. But that weren't me. God didn't see fit to give me those kind of folks. Me and my brother Pete." With slumped shoulders, Chet stared down at empty hands.

That look in Chet's eyes. Peyton had seen it before—in his own eyes. The boy had experienced hardship in his life—and at his young age. Desire built in Peyton. More than ever, he wanted to help him, but how—he didn't know. "Can you tell me about your brother?"

Chet pulled at his ear lobe. "Aww, nothing you'd care about."

`"Try me." Peyton gripped the kid's shoulders to face him. "You remind me of me once."

Chet dug the heel of his boot in the straw and then raised his voice. "I lived in San Antonio. I didn't have no pa." He huffed. "Only my mom and she was always gone to work." He frowned. "And my little brother Pete. He was the best kid brother anyone could ever have."

"Was?" Peyton lowered his voice. "Where's Pete now?"

Chet swallowed hard, as if trying to get control over his emotions. "I don't know for sure. Probably in foster care somewhere."

"Let's go into the barn." He started through the door, Chet following. He squeezed his eyes shut, rubbed his brow, and then opened his lids again. More than ever, he knew the truth. He wanted to help this kid and others like him. A desire which had lain dormant for a while began to take shape, squeezing his heart. A glimpse of his future flickered in his brain. He drew Chet farther into the barn. "I'm here to listen to you, not to judge. If I can help in any way, I will."

Chet stared at Peyton and pinched his lips together as if assessing Peyton's words. He cleared his voice. "I couldn't help what I done. My kid brother was hungry and there weren't no food in the fridge."

"What did you do?" Peyton whispered.

Chet stood in front of the sheep pen, the ewe cuddling her lamb in the clean straw. He stared straight ahead as if he existed in another time and place. "My friends told me I could make money selling cocaine, so me and Pete could eat. But the police caught me peddling and found out we were at home alone most of the time. They called in the social services, and since I was only sixteen and this was my first offense, they didn't charge me, but they put us in two different foster homes. One night, I ran off."

A stab of pain gouged Peyton's heart. "I'm sorry."

"I wanted to find Pete, but I had no idea where to look." Chet's voice sounded clogged and harsh. "I headed to the streets for a couple of weeks. Then I left town, hitching rides. I had no idea where I'd go. I wound up in Oakville and saw the notice at the grocery store."

"Notice?"

"For a ranch hand at the Ford ranch. Mr. Ford's a good man. He took me on and promised he'd help me get my GED. I lied about my age, but I'm planning to tell him the truth when I turn eighteen pretty soon." He gripped Peyton's arm and widened his eyes. "Hey, you ain't gonna tell him?"

Peyton raised his right hand. "It's not my place. I brought you into this conversation. You trusted me, and I can't tell him something you told me in confidence." Finally, the longing that had built inside Peyton before his loss re-emerged from the shadows of his heart. He and Sandra had talked about ways to help others, taking the prosperity given to him by the Lord and using it to invest in the lives of others. They hadn't had a clue what to do.

Had God set him here in this place at this time, to meet Chet and to train up Peyton to do God's will? Since tragedy had stripped away his growing family from him, he understood loss. There were younger boys who suffered the same. Why couldn't he help by providing a new family—a boys' ranch where they could find hope and belonging?

"Thanks, Peyton." Chet turned his back.

"No, I have to thank you."

Chet glanced around and frowned. "Thank me?"

"Yes. I have the direction I've been looking for."

Chet stared at him. "Direction?" He cleared his throat. "I don't get it."

"God willing, in time you will."

Using a manure fork, Erika tossed the horse droppings into the wheelbarrow. She sorted out the wet shavings and sprinkled baking soda around. Finally, she spread a new bale of wood shavings using her pitchfork.

She glanced at her watch. Twelve noon on Saturday and quitting time. She had the rest of the day to finish the historical novel she'd begun or even go shopping in Oakville.

But first she needed to bring the horses back to their pens. She untied Paint's reins from the barn door and patted his neck. "Your stall's nice and clean now. I bet you're ready for a break, too."

She smiled, remembering Dad's words the first time she'd spoken to her horse when she was seven. "You create a lasting bond with your animal when you talk to them." Since that day, she'd communicated with them as if they understood every word. She giggled. Of course, they did.

Erika returned each of the horses to their clean pens and gazed at the road leading to the entrance of the ranch and the main highway. Sunny skies and the balmy weather typical of this time of year coaxed her to explore the new boutique in downtown Oakville.

Once again, she drew her attention to the road running in front of the house and leading to town. Large rocks that her great grandfather had arranged years ago lined the paved surface on either side. But one rock had become dislodged from its original position and sat several feet within the road. She'd meant to remove the obstacle for over a year now—especially after last month when she almost ran into it with her car.

The equipment shed stood in front of the horse barn. Through the open door, she spotted the tractor. An idea seeped into her brain, and she headed toward the building.

The tractor with hydraulic forks would help her accomplish the job. Besides, her father would be proud of her for doing something no one else seemed to have time for.

Erika rushed into the shed and hopped up on the tractor. The gear shift and hydraulic controls in neutral, she depressed the clutch and turned the key. The hum of the engine delivered a rare sense of success, and she lifted her chin as she drove out the door.

The troublesome rock lay in the road about fifteen yards ahead. She revved the motor as she drew closer, ready to accomplish her job.

"Erika, Erika, stop." A masculine voice behind her yelled.

She brought the machine to a standstill and turned

around.

Jace raced toward her. He waved his arms in the air, still shouting.

Didn't he trust her to do a simple job? She hmphed. "What's the problem?" she shouted.

"The oil pan under the tractor, didn't you see it? We're changing the oil, and it's in a slow drip." Jace's face was fiery red with fury.

The slow realization of what had happened descended like raw eggs making an unhurried journey to her gut. She hadn't checked under the tractor. But then Jace hadn't told her he was changing the tractor's oil today.

"Erika." Her father arrived, his face as flushed as Jace's. "You need to learn that there are some things around this ranch that only your brothers and I should do. Please don't let that happen again. You almost ruined our tractor driving it with no oil."

Erika clasped her hands on her hips. "Communication seems to a problem around here. Had I been informed you were working on the tractor, this might not have happened. I suggest we post a work schedule on the bulletin board in your office."

"Could be a good idea." Dad gazed toward the tool shed as if seeking an answer there. With a shake of his head, he pulled his attention to her again. "Still, I don't want you working with the tractor."

"Why not?" Erika didn't like to argue with her father, yet she had to stand up for herself.

He sputtered. "Because I ... " Dad looked at her then turned to Jace. "Help me get the tractor back into the tool shed."

What had he meant to say? And who did he think

would use the tractor after he retired? She blew out a stream of air.

Erika walked slowly toward the house. Guess she'd get started on her novel, but would she be able to concentrate trying to figure out if Dad was being honest with her?

Chapter Six

Outside the bunkhouse, Peyton shaded his eyes against the bright sun. He fastened the top button on his western-style shirt he purchased at the box store in Oakville when he first arrived and looked around for the van. The aroma of newly mowed grass filled his lungs.

Mr. Ford waved from the driver's side of the economy-sized van, Mrs. Ford by his side. "Ready to go, Peyton?"

Peyton picked up his pace and slipped through the sliding doors and into the third row of seats next to Jace and Charlotte. He nodded to Austin and Mac in the middle section. No Chet. No Erika.

Shifting into gear, Mr. Ford inched past the tool shed and horse barn and glanced in the rearview mirror. "Glad you could make it today, Peyton."

Mrs. Ford turned in her seat to smile at him. "Erika will be along as well. She'll bring her own car. Sometimes, she likes to get out on her own on Sunday. We have some things planned if you're interested. A family picnic down on the Mesquite River after church and then a visit with Grandma and Grandpa. You're welcome to join us."

"Thanks. I'd like that. I appreciate you including your ranch hands in on family time."

Interesting. Erika hadn't mentioned any family traditions. Maybe as her mom said, Sunday was her day to go out on her own.

Mr. Ford pulled onto the main highway toward town. "My parents retired to Oakville about ten years ago and always love to see family."

"I'd like to meet them." Peyton stared at the back of Mr. Ford's head. He figured more than one generation of Fords had been ranchers. "You grew up on the Ford property?"

"Yep. Mom, Dad, and I lived in the house where Jace and Charlotte are now." He patted Mrs. Ford's arm. "My wife and I built our present home after we married. We figured we wanted a large family, and the old family house only had three bedrooms."

"Your house is beautiful. If I ever built one, I'd want all those windows with the outside view, as well." If he built a house? What were the chances? "The covered porch and exposed wooden beams are nice."

"Thanks." Mr. Ford glanced in his rearview mirror. "My grandfather, the kids' great grandfather, bought the ranch in the forties. I'm a third-generation rancher. Jace and Austin will make a fourth one day. Tim, as well, if he wants to leave Lubbock."

Peyton swiped a hand over his mouth. No mention of Erika. From what he'd observed, the barriers between Erika and Mr. Ford were likely as high as the fence around the north pasture.

Low growing bushes lined the two-lane road that wound around the typical Central Texas hill dotted with sage brush and cactus. Forging through two smaller hills, the highway made its way to the valley and the town of Oakville. Buildings, parks, and homes popped up as the van approached the town limits, probably a tenth the size of San Antonio.

Instead of turning toward downtown, Mr. Ford made a right onto a dirt road. The van jostled and bumped as they pulled up in front of a corral.

Peyton wrinkled his brow. The place looked like a ranch, not a church.

"This is it. Oakville Cowboy Church. Our congregation's focus is on reaching out to the ranchers, ranch hands, and their families. Of course, everyone is welcome. Not all our members work on a ranch. We have quite a few Oakville citizens attending here." Mr. Ford said.

Dust billowed up around the vehicle as they curved onto another dirt road, and then Erika's father parked in a large, grassy field in front of a sizable rustic-style building. "Peyton, ever attend a cowboy church before?" Mr. Ford cut the ignition and opened his door to get out.

Peyton plopped his hat on top of his head and adjusted the brim. "No, sir. First time this morning."

Less like a church, the red painted building looked like a barn with its rough-cut timber beams and high windows. He followed the others through the entrance and foyer and down an aisle separating rows of folding chairs, the inside space finally resembling a place of worship.

"We usually sit in front." Mrs. Ford smiled at him and continued down the aisle.

Erika sat in the fourth row, one seat from the middle aisle. She appeared to force a smile as the family crowded past her on the same row.

Peyton dropped into the empty chair next to the aisle. "This seat taken?" He hoped his quick smile would lighten the tension that hung in the air.

A grin crossed her face. "Saving it for you." She fiddled with her cell phone in her lap.

As the service progressed, each song led by the worship leader with his guitar lifted Peyton's frame of mind. Surely, the pastor's message about riding out the storms of life was meant for him.

He peeked at Erika for the tenth time. Her arms over her chest hinted at a protective shield she'd created. Didn't she like coming to church? Or was it something about her family? Peyton determined to find out.

Erika rose from her seat and followed the tall cowboy into the aisle. Sitting by him in church did her good. She lived and worked with her family six days a week. Face it, she needed a break.

Peyton's shoulders swayed as he ambled up the aisle. His jeans fit his slim hips flawlessly. He slid his Stetson on his head and stopped in the foyer. "Your parents are going to the river for a picnic. You going?"

She tapped her forehead. "They usually get upset when I don't go, but today, I'd like to take off on my own. Do a little shopping in Oakville. Grab some lunch in town. Want to come along?"

"Sure. I'd told your dad I'd go to the picnic, but I'm sure he'll understand if I change my mind. Besides, I need to pick up a few things at the drug store anyway." He glanced around the crowd of people. "Let me speak to your folks."

Erika followed him to the other side of the foyer where Dad and Mom talked to the pastor.

As the preacher moved on to another group of people, Peyton approached her father. "Mr. Ford. I appreciate the invitation to join you today, but I need to do some shopping. I'll go back to the ranch with Erika."

"I suppose she decided not to go to the picnic today." Dad looked over Peyton's shoulder at her. "Erika, don't you think you'd like to join us today and then visit with your grandparents? You know we only hold family events once a month of so."

Dad's glare sent a chill up her spine. It was as if her father wanted to control every part of her life. Sunday was her day off, after all. "Dad, not today. I'll visit Grandma and Grandpa another time."

A couple of people close by stopped their conversations and stared at them.

Mom nudged Dad. "We'd better leave now."

Face hot, Erika walked out behind them. She whispered to Peyton. "I'm sorry you had to get in on some of our family drama."

"Hey, no problem." Out in the parking lot, Peyton folded his long legs into the passenger seat of her car.

She headed out to the main road. "How did you like church?"

He shifted on the passenger seat. "Your pastor preaches from the Bible. I enjoyed it. What about you?"

"I'll be honest. Most of the time I don't understand what he's talking about. I suppose I go because I'm expect to attend." Besides, she felt as if her father wanted her to commit to something she wasn't ready to embrace. To join his church because that's what the Ford's did. She signaled to turn at the first stop light.

"I'm not an expert, but if I can help you understand any of the scriptures, I'll be happy to."

"Thanks, I'll think about that." His simple comment didn't sound pushy like when Dad talked to her about religion. "But right now, let's have lunch."

"Excellent. I'm starved."

Five minutes later, she parked in front of Oakville Oasis. "How's this?"

"As long as they have food, I'm fine." Peyton's silvery laugh helped to erase some of the tension from only moments ago.

Peyton had to admit, he'd welcomed the turkey, avocado, and goat cheese panini. Not that the meals at the ranch weren't delicious, but eating at a trendy restaurant was nice for a change.

"You want to see the waterfall at our little city park?" Erika glanced at him and then back to the road.

"Sure. I haven't had time to explore much." And a chance to spend time with the good-looking woman in the driver's seat.

Erika parked and clicked the locks on her car. "Down this path and on the left. It's a short walk."

They strolled past oaks, elms, and colorful crape myrtle that lined the dirt path.

Hands covering their mouths as if revealing secrets, two teenaged girls walked past. A jogger in black and white shorts sprinted around Erika and Peyton.

Erika picked up a colorful rock and then tossed it beside the path. "Tell me more about yourself, Peyton."

How much did he want her to know? Hadn't he come to the ranch in search of a new life? "I went to college and worked in Dallas for a while. What about you?"

The look she gave him clearly showed she'd wanted more. She shrugged. "High school in Oakville and then I attended the university to become an elementary teacher."

"But that didn't come to pass." Peyton glanced ahead at the winding path. No sign of a waterfall.

"I finally got it figured out. My parents had wanted me to go into education, but I decided my passion was to live and work on the ranch."

He snickered. "So, you had rather wrestle with ornery sheep then a bunch of little kids."

"That's about it." She laughed. "Although the rams tend to put up a fight on occasion." Erika picked up her pace. "The falls are right around here." She pointed to the left. At the curve, she glanced at him. "Any special women in your life?"

Peyton combed his fingers through his hair. How to answer? "Long story. Another time. I'll ask you the same." There, he'd dodged another question he didn't want to answer now.

"I used to have a crush on a guy named Hank, but he didn't have time for me."

"He must've been crazy." How could any guy not be into her?

Erika raised her eyebrows. "Sometimes I wonder what would've happened if I'd taken a teaching job in

San Antonion or Austin? To make a major lifestyle change would be scary. But you did it—leaving the city and settling on a ranch. How did you manage it?"

How did he do it? Only with God's help. "A lot happened. A lot of regret. Right now, isn't the best time …"

"Sorry, I asked the wrong question."

"One of these days I'll be ready to talk about it." The more he got to know Erika, the easier it would be to trust her.

The path bent to the left. "Up this way. You'll love this."

Ahead, the foliage became dense, palm branches, moss, and ferns decorating the spot. In the distance, layers of limestone rose from behind the trees, and a veil of water cascaded over the rocks.

"The creeks and rivers are low right now, but there'll be more water later in the summer." Erika took a few steps nearer the falls.

Several ornate, white benches faced the waterfall.

White hair and cane, an elderly man occupied one, his gaze obviously on the flowing water.

Peyton nodded toward one of the benches. "That older gentleman up there seems like he's enjoying the view."

Erika glanced in the direction he'd indicated. "Yes, lots of our senior population enjoy the park." She frowned and took a step forward. "Hmm. He looks like—"

The old man rubbed his head and tried to push up from the bench. As he stood, he swayed and then fell onto the ground.

Erika screamed. "Grandpa!" She raced toward the

man. "Oh, Grandpa, what happened?" Her voice shook with her emotion.

Peyton dialed 9-1-1 and gave the attendant the information. He rushed to Erika's side as she stared at the man lying on his side on the ground. "Your grandfather?"

"Yes, he loves this park. He comes here frequently. I didn't realize he wasn't well." Erika dropped to her knees and patted his cheek.

Peyton gently rolled Erika's grandfather onto his back. He propped up his legs on a wide, smooth rock, and loosened his belt. "Sir, sir. Can you hear me?"

The man groaned and tried to sit up.

Erika gasped and gripped her throat. "Oh, Peyton. He isn't Grandpa."

The man groaned. "Guess I forgot to take my blood pressure med … "

"I called EMS. They'll be here soon."

The elderly man shook his head. "I'm okay."

Erika slid down beside the guy and picked up his hand. "He looks so much like … "

Peyton helped the man up onto the bench. "When was the last time you took your pressure meds?"

"Guess it's been a month or so." The man squeezed Erika's hand.

"Well, there you go." Peyton squatted down in front of the man. Erika's grandfather or no, he needed to take care of himself.

Erika stood by as the paramedics lifted the man to

the gurney.

"We'll get him to the hospital and notify his family. The doc will probably keep him overnight for observation, but I think he'll be fine. That is if we can get him to take his hypertension medication."

Did Grandpa take any meds, and if so, did he keep up with them? She intended to ask at the next visit.

Grandpa.

The thought hit her. Her grandfather was getting older. One of these days he might … She could barely finish her thoughts. Die. Was she ready for that? Was Grandpa? Where would he go if he died tomorrow? Strange how seeing this elderly man sparked the notion.

Erika glanced at Peyton. "We don't usually have such eventful happenings at the park."

Peyton rubbed the back of his neck with his hand. "I'm glad the other man got help, but I'm sure grateful he wasn't your grandfather."

"Me, too. I can't tell you how scared I got when I thought my own grandfather lay on the ground by the waterfall." Erika sank down onto the park bench.

The question continued to burn in her mind. What *would* happen to him when he died? What would happen to *her*, and did it matter?

Chapter Seven

Monday morning, outside the tool shed, Peyton glanced from Chet standing next to him to the boss.

Mr. Ford folded his arms as he ambled toward them. "I want you two to go up to the north pasture and replace a couple of rotten posts." He eyed Chet and glanced back to Peyton.

Peyton smiled. "Will do." Those videos he watched last night would help.

Mr. Ford lifted a gas-driven auger from its place and set it in the back of the flatbed truck.

"You'll also need a saw." He returned to the shed and retrieved a chainsaw. "Make sure you attach those ratchet straps to the anchor points on the bed of the truck." He secured both tools, tightening the straps.

"You got it." Peyton hopped into the truck, Chet in the passenger seat.

"Okay, men. See you at dinner." Mr. Ford headed toward his office at the big house.

The truck leaned and bounced as they moved along on the dirt road. Peyton frowned. "Mr. Ford said the portion of rotten fence is a couple of yards past the eastward bend." Though the video had been informative, would they be able to perform the actual job?

"Don't worry, Peyton. We got this." Chet pulled out his cell phone. "Mr. Ford sent me a couple of pictures."

"Depending on you, buddy." Peyton steered to the right with the curve in the road. "I missed you at church yesterday."

Chet cleared his throat. "Yeah. Like I said, going to church isn't my thing."

Peyton hoped that one day attending church would be *his thing*. If Peyton hadn't had faith in God these past couple of years … He wanted the same for Chet, but no sense in putting pressure on the kid. Maybe … in time, Chet would see his need for God. "So, what are you planning to do after you get your GED?"

Chet sighed. "Truthfully, I've always loved animals. I'd like to get an associate in animal science, maybe."

Peyton slapped Chet's shoulder. "Proud of you, buddy. I'd like to help you in any way I can."

"You would?" Chet lowered his voice. "Why would you even care?"

He glanced toward the kid to see his reaction. "I was fortunate to have a father who did. But if Dad wasn't around, I would've appreciated knowing someone else was concerned about me." Peyton pulled up alongside the fence as the railing took a turn toward the east.

Chet shook his head. "He may have shown you love but … " Chet shoved the passenger door open.

Peyton exited the truck and made a mental note. He needed to go easy on Chet. The poor kid was filled with anger.

The two wooden posts about five feet apart that

supported the wire section of the fence wiggled as Peyton moved them each back and forth.

Chet glanced at the picture on his phone. "Yep, these are the ones."

After removing the equipment from the truck, Peyton cut the first post with the battery-powered chainsaw as the video had demonstrated. He removed the rotten post and set the section to one side, the bottom part swarming with termites.

Chet grasped the saw. "I went with Mac when he repaired a fence in the other pasture before you showed up at the ranch. That's about how he did it. Let me take out the next one, and you can clean out the hole with the auger."

"Sounds like a plan." Peyton gave an inward smile. The boy demonstrated leadership skills today, for which Peyton was glad.

Peyton secured the first post and then used the auger to make the second hole after Chet removed the rotten one.

Something about thirty yards toward the east caught his eye. A lump of some kind. He tightened his fist. Not another lamb fallen prey to a coyote. Erika wouldn't want to hear the news. "I'll be back in a minute. I need to check something."

"No problem. I'll finish the last post and get the equipment in the truck while you're doing that." Chet grasped the saw.

Peyton walked alongside the fence nearer the object. About five feet away, a white, flat granite rock lay partially within the cover of a bush. His slain sheep wasn't an animal but a rock. He scratched the back of his neck, firmed his lips, and returned to the truck.

Thankfully, he wouldn't have to tell Erika he'd found another dead lamb.

"Guess we're done." Chet walked toward the passenger side of the vehicle.

"Yep. I think that'll do it." Peyton turned to admire the job they'd done on the fence. Mr. Ford would be pleased. He climbed into the driver's seat to head back to the ranch house. Mrs. Ford would be serving dinner soon, and his appetite let him know he was ready for a meal. "Good job, today, Chet." Using positive reinforcement with the boy was important, something he'd likely not received in his short life.

"Yeah, sure." Chet stared at his cell phone.

Not the answer Peyton had hoped for. Did the kid not believe him, or maybe compliments made him feel uncomfortable?

The truck bounced and bumped, creating a curtain of dirt surrounding the truck.

A thought also bounced into Peyton's brain. "Did you secure the auger and saw when you put the equipment in the back."

Chet glanced up from his cell phone. "Huh? Oh. Yeah."

"Great." Peyton brought the truck to a stop at the tool shed. Return the equipment, and it would be quitting time.

Mr. Ford walked out of the sheep barn and toward them. "How did it go?"

Chet threw his shoulders back. "We done a good job, sir."

The rancher smiled and headed toward the truck's flatbed. His pleasant expression morphed to a frown. "Where's the chainsaw? And why's the auger not secured with a bungie cord and dangling near the edge of the truck? It could've fallen off onto the road," he huffed, "like I'm afraid the chainsaw did."

Peyton's mouth fell open. "What?" He marched closer to the back of the truck.

Mr. Ford scowled. "You forgot to secure the tools. I even demonstrated how to attach them. " He lifted the ratchet belts over his head. "The saw is probably somewhere on the road."

Peyton sucked in a breath, the situation now clear.

"I'm surprised, Peyton." Mr. Ford frowned at him. "I expected better of you. Head on back and fetch my saw out of the dirt."

Peyton opened his mouth to protest and to tell the man Chet was responsible for the accident. Instead, he pressed his lips together. This one time he'd protect the boy, and he prayed they'd both learn a lesson. "Yes, sir." Peyton eyed Chet and jumped into the passenger seat. "Get in." His command was gruffer than he intended.

Chet's eyes were wide, and he shook his head. "I'm sorry. I guess I better pay more attention. I didn't fasten the strap, but he thinks it's your fault."

Peyton turned back the way they'd come. He hoped his lecture would sink into that teenaged brain. "Chet, we need to respect equipment that doesn't belong to us. Mr. Ford pays good money for his tools. Treat his stuff the same way you'd take care of your own possessions."

Chet hung his head and nodded. "Gosh. I'm really sorry. I'll do better next time." He scrubbed a hand over his mouth. "I've never had someone take the blame for me before. I don't know why you'd want to do something like that. But, thank you."

Peyton finished off his serving of chicken enchilada casserole. He stuck his spoon into the dish of flan and then glanced at Chet. He couldn't remember when the young guy had been speechless at dinner when he ordinarily spoke about wanting to learn to use a rope, or how good the food was, or the arrival of a new lamb.

Chet fiddled with his food and dipped his head.

Peyton sighed. The kid felt guilty, but he had to learn the hard way, like everybody else.

Someone tapped Peyton on his shoulder. "Can I speak to you in the living room?" Jace towered over him.

Peyton pushed his plate to one side. "Sure, just finished." From Jace's expression, Erika's brother didn't want to talk about the weather.

Mac lifted a brow, shrugged, and then sipped his coffee.

In the empty living room, Peyton folded his arms over his chest and turned to peer at Jace's scowling face. "What's up?"

"It's more like what went down." Jace tightened his jaws. "Don't you have enough sense to tie an auger to the back of a truck when you're traveling over a rough road?" His face was as red as his Texas Tech T-shirt.

Peyton's heart pounded a little harder at the deliberate confrontation from Jace. "Fortunately, the chain saw fell into a pile of soft dirt. There was no damage when I retrieved the tool." He held firm to his decision not to bring Chet into the unfortunate accident.

Jace drew closer to Peyton, and his nostrils flared. "My father is a kind and generous man. If I thought for one moment one of his amateur employees was taking advantage of his good nature ... " Jace grit his teeth.

Why was this guy so aggressive? Peyton held up two hands. "It was an accident. I'm sure it won't happen again." Peyton didn't care to get grilled by Erika's angry brother. He turned toward the back door and headed to the bunkhouse. A moment to cool off would do him good.

"Peyton, wait up." Mac called to him from behind.

Peyton slowed his pace. Might as well hear what Mac had to say. Hopefully, he wouldn't decide to scold him, too.

Mac blew out a breath of air. "While you were gone, Chet explained about what happened. Though he didn't say much during dinner, I guess he figured he'd better speak up. You took the heat for him, he said."

Peyton nodded and continued on. Even though he liked and respected Mac, he needed a break from the subject right now.

Mac's footsteps grew louder, and he slapped Peyton's shoulder. "Don't pay any attention to Jace. He comes off high-and-mighty ever so often." The ranch hand walked by Peyton's side. "And I got one more thing to say. Your actions today probably did the kid good—offering him a little grace."

Chapter Eight

Erika tightened her fists, her nails biting into the palms of her hands. She clicked the locks on her car, settled into the driver's seat, and started the motor. Sure, she didn't mind going to Oakville to get groceries for Mom, but someday she'd be in charge of purchases from the feed store or the tractor supply instead of her brothers.

From the vegetable garden on the east side of the house, Peyton waved and walked up to her car, a basket of carrots, spinach, and lettuce in hand.

She lowered her glass on the passenger side.

Peyton propped his elbows on the window's edge. "I need to discuss some ranch business with you—something that happened yesterday. Do you have a minute?"

"Sure. You want to ride with me to town?" Once again, her father hadn't shared a detail about the Ford ranch. Strange that she'd have to hear family business from Peyton, a new hire.

"I'll be right back if you can wait a second." He strode to the porch and set the basket on the side entrance to the kitchen. With long, even strides, making her face heat as she imagined the leg muscles rippling under his jeans, he returned, trekking toward her car.

Erika unlocked the passenger door. "Mom's sending me to do some grocery shopping. We can talk on the way."

"Thanks. I finished up my last job for today so I'm free to go." He crawled into the passenger's seat and whistled some tune she hadn't heard before.

Erika passed the Ford ranch sign at the entrance and drove onto the main road. "So, tell me what happened?" She braced to hear what he had to say—whatever Dad didn't think necessary to tell his daughter.

"Look, Erika. I'm not trying to tell tales or gossip about what goes on around the ranch. I need your advice as to how to handle this kind of situation in the future." Peyton rubbed the back of his neck.

Warmth radiated through her chest. He trusted her and wanted her advice. "Sure."

Peyton fiddled with his shirt button. "Chet and I had a minor problem with the equipment when we returned from the north pasture yesterday. Your brother, Jace, told me in no uncertain terms what he thought about the situation."

"What did he say?"

"That I should've known better. I do know better, but I didn't tell him the whole story, and he assumed I was an idiot." He sat up straight. "I'm not objecting to a tongue-lashing if I deserve it, but in this case, I don't believe I did. Who is boss around here, your brother or your father?"

"Definitely my father." She reached to pat his hand. "Don't worry about it. Dad didn't mention any kind of problem so I guess he wasn't concerned." Though, as of late, her father wasn't in the habit of sharing much at all with her. "Jace is unreasonable and loses his temper on occasion."

"I get it." Peyton cleared his throat. "Over and done with. Thanks, Erika, that was helpful."

A tingle ran along her spine. Peyton had trusted her with a ranch situation where he needed clarification. He wouldn't have asked if he didn't respect her opinion. "Anytime."

In town, she turned down Main Street toward S & L Grocery. "After shopping, I'd like to visit my grandparents if you want to go along. I missed seeing them Sunday."

"Sounds fine. Your father mentioned his parents and how he grew up on the ranch."

"You'll like them. They don't get out as much as they used to, so I visit them whenever I can." Finally, Peyton would meet some of her family who actually appreciated her.

With the frozen items in the cooler she'd stowed in the trunk, Erika pulled up in front of the familiar red brick house shaded by the lofty oak trees so prevalent in Oakville. Spending time with Grandpa Martin and Grandma Theresa seemed like taking a journey into the past. A step back in time where she could learn more about her roots. And enjoy their affection and affirmation.

She approached the one-story house and tapped at the door, Peyton behind her. "Grandpa, Grandma, it's Erika."

The sweet, herbal smell of the lavender bushes in the front flower bed brought back memories of Grandma's scent when Erika was a small girl. Her grandmother—always ready for a hug or to read her a story.

The screen door squeaked open, and Grandma opened her arms wide. "Oh, my sweetheart. I'm so happy to see you." She glanced at Peyton. "Come in, both of you."

The aroma of fresh gingerbread filled the air. In the small living room with the overstuffed sofa, paisley carpet, and recliner, she rushed to give Grandpa a hug. She nodded toward Peyton. "Grandma, Grandpa, this is Peyton Langley. He's the new ranch hand Dad hired."

Grandpa approached with his hand extended to shake Peyton's. "Nice to meet you, young fellow."

Peyton's smile couldn't be wider. No doubt, he felt comfortable around older people. He pumped Grandpa's hand. "Pleasure's all mine. And thanks for the compliment. Sometimes I don't feel so young."

Grandma's eyes seem to sparkle with joy. "Sit down, you two. I pulled some hot gingerbread from the oven a few minutes ago. Would you like a piece and a cup of coffee?"

Peyton's face lit. "You betcha." He relaxed into the easy chair across from Grandpa's recliner.

Erika smiled at Grandma. "Can I help?"

Grandma shooed her with the back of her hand. "You sit and talk to your grandfather. I'm blessed to see you and to meet the new employee."

The opportunity to speak to Grandpa had arrived. Erika leaned forward in the chair. "Peyton and I ran into a man in the park last week. The guy passed out because he didn't take his meds properly. Peyton called 9-1-1." She bit her lip. "I sure wouldn't want that to happened to you."

Grandpa laughed. "Don't worry, my sweet girl. I only take one medication. I'm as fit as a flea."

Nothing to do but take Grandpa at his word.

Within ten minutes, Grandma returned with a tray of desserts and coffee. Why did life always seem simpler at her grandparents' house? Erika leaned back on the couch and slowly exhaled.

Peyton forked a bite of gingerbread into his mouth and turned to Grandpa in his favorite easy chair. "I understand you ran the ranch before Erika's father."

Erika smiled. Clearly, Peyton enjoyed her grandparent's peaceful home as much as she did.

"Yes." Grandpa set the recliner in motion. "Theresa and I made our living on that ranch and raised our children there. We had our share of problems, but looking back now, the Lord saw us through and blessed us."

Peyton set his plate on the coffee table. "Erika didn't mention any other children besides her father."

Grandpa squeezed his eyes shut and opened them again as he rubbed his forehead. "I'm sorry. I usually don't talk about our Rebekah. She passed away when she was ten."

Grandma turned to Peyton. "Grandpa and I will always miss her."

"Every time I hear about my Aunt Rebekah, I want to cry." Erika's voice broke. "I've seen old pictures of her. She was a beautiful little girl."

Grandma folded her hands in her lap and glanced at Peyton. "You see, her loss caused our family more grief than I can say, especially Erika's father. I've seen him actually get up and walk out of the room when her name is mentioned."

Peyton took a sip of coffee. "If I may ask, what happened?"

"Our girl fell off her horse one day when he got spooked by a rattler," Grandma said. "She hit her head on a rock and … " Grandma took a deep breath and stared straight ahead.

Peyton shifted in the chair. "I'm sorry if I brought up an uncomfortable subject."

Grandpa waved one hand in front of him. "Son, you didn't do anything wrong."

"Well, this visit certainly isn't a loss when we can be together." Grandma patted Erika's hand. "Let's find another subject to talk about."

Grandma. Erika could always count on her to navigate the obstacles in life and move on.

Grandma clasped her hands as if in prayer. "Let's tell Peyton about our annual bar-b-que that helps to fund the boys' home in Oakville. The event is coming up here in a month."

After dinner, Peyton moseyed around the big house to the swinging chair-for-two hanging by ropes under the giant oak. The night air would help to clear his head.

When he'd first arrived at the ranch, he only wanted freedom from his thoughts, from his emotions, his memories. He'd had enough difficulties in the past to last a lifetime. But the previous couple of days were more eventful than he might've imagined.

Peyton scooted onto the swing. A cacophony of night sounds blended into one, and a chorus of crickets and frogs gave a stellar performance. Yet the serenade didn't prevent the barrage of new thoughts from invading his mind.

Jace's angry face glared once more, but Peyton would protect Chet again if he had to. The kid needed someone to stand up for him—to go easy on him.

Then learning Erika's aunt had died a regretful death touched him. He'd read the heartache on her face as well as that of her grandparents. He'd lost a close relative and understood the sadness they all held.

"Mind if I sit?" He'd barely heard Erika's words. Her tone was different from earlier today when they first arrived at her grandmother's. It wasn't hard to understand why no one had mentioned Rebekah before. They all had been affected by the loss, even a niece who'd never met her.

He scooted over and patted the wooden, swinging seat. "There's nothing like the cool evening air to refresh you." He smoothed his hand over hers and then pulled his away, trying to ignore the spark buzzing up his arm. He only meant to let her know he was her friend. But he didn't want her to get the wrong idea.

She glanced at him and then gazed at her hands she'd moved to her lap. "Talking about Aunt Rebekah always seems to get me down."

"I'm sorry," he whispered.

"Especially concerning Dad. He never seems to want to talk about her, to tell me about his memories of her as a child. What games they played or what were their favorite books. I've asked him, and he changes the subject. Honestly, Peyton, I've never felt free to approach Dad with any topics besides the weather and the ranching chores he wants me to do."

"That's tough." Peyton gave a push with one boot to set the swing in motion. "Death is a painful subject—especially for those of us who're left. I've tasted loss myself." Peyton rested his elbows on his knees.

Erika smoothed her hand over his shoulder and then removed her fingers. "Do you want to talk about it."

Peyton gulped. He'd never want to think about what happened again much less talk about those times. "No," he managed to say.

Erika kicked off her house shoes and crawled into bed.

The moon radiated silver beams through her window and onto her trophy and awards shelf. Memories from childhood rushed into her mind—recognition of her 4H projects and medals she'd won—the achievements and accomplishments.

Riding the pasture on Paint and her hair blowing in the breeze were at the top of her teenaged recollection. Brushing her horse each evening, polishing her saddle—she'd never forget.

She relaxed against the satin smoothness of her pillow and then another remembrance breezed into her mind—Peyton's warmth next to her in the swing tonight. Sitting by his side seemed so natural, as if she belonged there. No guy had ever made her feel the way he did.

Though she didn't want to admit it, his touch had sent tingles up her hand. She wouldn't tell him, but she'd wished he hadn't moved his warm, large fingers from hers.

She flopped over on her side and closed her eyes, but would sleep come? She recalled Peyton's words. He'd said he'd suffered the loss of someone as well, obviously someone who meant a lot to him. But who? Would he ever want to talk about his mysterious past?

Chapter Nine

Still mulling over last night's conversation with Erika, Peyton swallowed the last sip of coffee and headed out the front door of the ranch house. Maybe he'd share his past with her someday, but not now. He wasn't ready.

Peyton tramped across the grass to the tool shed. His first job for today—change the light bulb at the top of the horses' barn, and he needed the extension ladder. Inside the shed, the infamous circular saw sat on the shelf to the left. No major damage. But he'd learned a lesson. Next time, he'd inspect Chet's work.

He turned around at the sound of footsteps.

"Morning, Peyton." Mr. Ford's smile said he hadn't held any animosity concerning the mishap two days ago.

"Morning. Where do you keep those light bulbs for the outside fixtures?"

His boss motioned to a shelf toward the back of the shed. "Over there." He cleared his voice. "I understand Jace came on a little strong the other day. He's protective of the ranch, and it shows."

Peyton scratched his head. Nice gesture from the boss. "I get it. No problem. Chet and I will be more careful in the future."

"Yeah, about Chet." Mr. Ford replaced a nail puller from its place on the peg board. "I overheard you talking to him in the sheep barn the other day."

Did the boss approve or disapprove of what he'd said? He couldn't tell from the man's expression. Peyton met him eye to eye. "He's had a rough start."

"You'll get to meet other kids like him at the bar-b-que."

Peyton let out the breath he'd held. Mr. Ford wanted to serve needy boys like Peyton longed to do. "I'm looking forward to it."

The boss turned to him, a twinkle in his eye. "I figured out what else you did that day."

Peyton stiffened his shoulders. "What do you mean?"

"Been doing some thinking and came to a conclusion. Chet was responsible for securing the equipment in the back of the truck, and you accepted the blame for him when he neglected to take care of his responsibilities. I figure you wouldn't make a mistake like not tying down the tools."

Peyton lifted both palms in the air. So, the boss guessed right. But no matter. Chet or he would never make that mistake again. "No big deal."

Mr. Ford grinned. "Moving on to changing the light bulb. The extension ladder's on that wall." He nodded toward the opposite section of the tool shed from the bulbs. "You've used one before, right?"

Peyton nodded. "Sure. I used to help my father make minor repairs. We painted the entire house once—just the two of us."

"Good. Be careful to secure the wrung locks. If you

don't, the extension could collapse in on itself, and the ladder could fall over." Mr. Ford turned to walk out of the shed.

"Right." Ladder and bulb in hand, he passed the building where Mr. Ford stored his tractors, the ATV, and the livestock trailer. He'd wanted a challenging job to prove to Mr. Ford his capability on the ranch. And to keep his mind off Peru and the past. Today he'd gotten his wish.

The outside wall of the wooden structure that housed the horses was a good twenty-four feet to the roof. Peyton raised the extensions, secured the wrung locks, and propped the ladder against the outside wall.

At the top, he unscrewed the bulb and installed the new one within the gooseneck fixture. Success. He stepped down to the rung below him.

The ladder wobbled and swayed to the left.

What? He gripped the rung above him. Gravity assumed command. Nothing he could do to stop the trajectory of the contraption. He held his breath as he plummeted to the ground.

Agony knifed through his fingers as the hard surface met his hip. He ripped his hand from between two metal rungs. "Argh." The anguish of tearing flesh.

He sat up and lifted to one knee. Pain shot through his ribs.

"Peyton." Erika screamed and raced toward him from somewhere. "Are you okay?" She knelt down beside him.

Peyton tied to roll to one side and moaned with the pain.

She touched his shoulder. "The top extension of the ladder collapsed. Then the whole thing fell over, taking you with it."

Peyton groaned and rubbed his side. He'd done everything Mr. Ford had told him. What could've gone wrong? His hip hurt but nothing like his right hand. Blood streamed down his fingers.

"Looks like your fingers got caught between two rungs." Erika moved closer and examined his injury. "Can you move your fingers?"

Peyton breathed in a deep breath and wiggled them. "Yes."

"Good. No broken bones."

He pushed up from the ground to stand. Pain stabbed his right side again.

"Wait. Are you sure you're okay."

"Yes. I'm good." He couldn't sit there and act like a helpless child. He needed to shake it off.

Erika lay her hand on his shoulder. "Stay put one more minute. I'm going to grab a towel from the kitchen to wrap around your hand—to stop the bleeding. And then I'm taking you to the urgent care."

Peyton shook his head. Women. But she meant well.

A minute later, Erika returned with a clean kitchen towel and folded it around his hand, securing the makeshift bandage with some sticky tape. "The bleeding has stopped, but now let me get you to the doctor in Oakville—to check you out."

Pain inundated Peyton's body. He wasn't a wimp, but the truth of what happened, a twenty-foot fall, convinced him. He'd go. "Okay. Guess it wouldn't hurt."

Erika slipped her shoulder under his arm as he stood to his feet. "I got you. We can go in my car."

The feel of her warm body supporting his brought memories of another time and another woman. Her velvety, soft skin next to his—

Hurt shot through him again, jarring his mind as abruptly as the fall.

Mr. Ford rushed toward them from his office. "What happened?" He glanced from Peyton to the ladder on its side. "The rung locks aren't attached. Did you try to go up the ladder without securing them?" He tightened his lips into a firm line.

The boss's accusation shamed Peyton, like the times his father corrected him as a teen. "No, sir." He murmured. "I made sure to latch them."

Erika huffed and continued steering them in the direction of his car. "Dad, he needs medical attention. I'm taking him to Oakville."

Mr. Ford shook his head, as if disgusted. "All right. I'll come with you."

"No. I'll be fine." Erika trudged closer to her car, Peyton in tow.

Relieved Mr. Ford didn't come with them, Peyton eased into the passenger seat of Erika's vehicle, same place he sat yesterday when they went into town for groceries. Sure, he hurt, but had he brought the accident on himself? No. He'd made sure to latch the rung locks. Then what happened?

Erika sneaked a peek at Peyton as she pulled away from the clinic parking lot and onto the main road back to the ranch.

Head in his good hand, he closed his eyes, exhaling a breath, and sighed.

"Two broken ribs isn't fun. Since your hand lacerations were deep, I'm glad we got you to emergency care. Good thing the nurse gave you the tetanus shot and extra bandages."

"Yeah."

Not much response from him, but the poor guy hurt. "How's your pain level? Those meds the doctor prescribed should kick in soon."

He gripped his head again. "I'm fine."

"Men." Erika picked up speed after she rounded a curve. "You all say *fine* when you really hurt like crazy."

Peyton stretched one leg in front of him. "What bothers me the most is your father thinks I was negligent about setting up the ladder." He muttered something she couldn't understand.

"I'm sure my father will consider the ladder's age. He shouldn't have allowed you to climb up on it anyway."

He nodded and groaned, resting his head in his hand.

"I'll make sure Dad knows that the doc said to refrain from work for a couple of days. Then do light chores for about three weeks."

Peyton furrowed his brows and huffed. "Ranch hands don't do light work. He could lay me off."

"Peyton!" She raised her voice. "How fair do you think that is? Of course, he's not going to fire you. Why are you so tense about pleasing my father?" Was it related to his secret past? Ironically, he reminded her of how she'd become so concerned about Dad's opinions.

"I, I like this job and need to stay here for a while." Peyton gazed toward the passenger window, lost somewhere in his past.

After fifteen minutes, Erika turned in at the gate.

As she drove up, Dad walked out of his office and approached the passenger side of her car. He opened the door as Peyton struggled out.

Erika walked around and supported him once again. "He needs to rest. Let me get him to the bunkhouse, and I'll give you a report about what the doctor said."

Peyton backed away from her. "I'm fine." He glanced at Dad. "If I could lay down for a half hour, I can get back to work."

Dad shook his head. "No way. I inspected the ladder, and you were right. That thing is old, and the rung locks were worn. You may have put them in place, but they worked themselves out of position. I've ordered a new ladder." He combed his hand through his hair and cleared his throat. "You weren't at fault. I'm so sorry, Peyton, about the fall. I'm to blame. You're going on light duty for a while."

Peyton shook his head from side to side. "No, that's—"

"I'm the boss around here." Dad grinned.

Erika supported Peyton's bulk through the door of the bunkhouse. She leaned over him and eased him onto the bed. "Need me to take off your boots?"

Peyton sighed. "I don't like to admit being helpless, but my ribs say yes for a few more days until the pain lessens."

Tugging his boots, she slipped them off and set them next to the bed.

"Thank you. Maybe I can return the favor one day."

"What?" She laughed. "I hope not. I don't want any broken ribs."

Peyton tapped his forehead with his left hand and blew out a breath. "I mean … you know."

She lifted his legs onto the bed and smiled. "I do." She spread a blanket over him, walked toward the outer door, and then turned again to glance at him.

He'd laid his head on the pillow and closed his eyes. A slight frown on his brow, he attempted to turn sideways and rolled on his back again. He bit down on his lower lip.

"Get some rest, Peyton." She closed the door behind her.

Her father was a caring man. His apology to Peyton showed his true nature. Why then was he so distant with her?

Erika started toward her father's office, but stopped. Not today. She'd try to engage him in a deeper conversation some other time. Maybe she'd find a way to bring up Aunt Rebekah.

Chapter Ten

Peyton hobbled around the corner of the ranch house. The last four days had offered needed rest, but his ribs told him he wasn't ready for strenuous ranch work yet. He glanced at his phone. Almost time for the staff meeting. He opened the office door and shuffled in.

Mr. Ford looked up from his desk. Framed and on the wall behind him was a large family portrait.

Peyton glanced at the painting. "Great picture."

"I hired an artist to do it the year Erika turned fourteen. She had a little trouble sitting still." Mr. Ford chuckled.

A pretty, teenaged Erika stared back at him from the wall. She'd grown into a beautiful woman now. "Your mom and dad, Mrs. Ford, and all the children." Peyton gave a thumbs up. One day, he wanted a family, a wife and lots of kids …

Peyton stared a little longer at the young Erika, grinning to himself. Even then she displayed that independent spirit he saw in her now. He sank into one of the three chairs opposite the desk.

Hats removed, Mac, Jace, and Chet moseyed into the office and sat in front of Mr. Ford's desk on the couch next to the chairs.

Behind them, Austin plastered his hair down with one hand and plopped into a seat next to Jace.

Mr. Ford glanced at his watch. "Everyone's here except Erika." His smile looked more like a smirk.

Seated at his desk, Mr. Ford glanced at Peyton. "I noticed you're favoring your side. How's the pain level?"

Peyton didn't want to sound like a complainer. "The pain killers are helping. I change the bandage on my hand every day, and ice my ribs. Should be back to normal work in a couple more weeks."

"That's fine." He thumbed through a stack of papers on his desk.

Erika rushed into the office from the inside entrance, breathing fast. She took a seat next to Austin. "Sorry. Got caught up in the sheep barn."

Did Peyton imagine Mr. Ford's jaw tensing?

"All right. Let's get started." Mr. Ford tapped his pen on the desk. He looked around the room. "I'll be honest with you all. If we can't bring in more revenue with the sale of wool this spring and summer, the ranch is in trouble."

Erika gasped. "Are you saying we'd have to sell the property?"

Her father raised his palm. "Let's not go that far yet. With a lot of prayer and hard work, we may be able to increase sales, perhaps explore more avenues for marketing. But at this rate, we can only hold on another year or two."

Jace lifted his index finger. "What about purchasing more ewes and a few more rams? We have plenty of acreage to support them."

"That's an idea but as you know, the price of sheep is rising. We don't have the revenue to acquire more animals at this point." The boss rose from behind his desk and faced the group, resting on the edge of his desk. "I'm not trying to panic anyone. I'm merely saying let's put in our best effort." Mr. Ford ran his fingers through his thinning hair. "Okay, folks, get to work." He turned to Peyton. "If you can stay a few minutes, I'd like to discuss your duties."

The others walked out of the office, Jace eyeing Peyton with a suspicious stare.

"Sir, if you need to lay me off for a while, especially in light of the financial difficulties you spoke about—"

"No, no, Peyton. I have an idea." A slow smile crossed his boss's lips. "You have a background in business. I have a feeling you're exactly the employee I need right now."

Peyton sat up straight in his chair. He could envision where Mr. Ford was going with this. "What do you have in mind?"

"I'm sorry about the accident, but putting you on light work couldn't have come at a better time. Do you think you can use a computer with that bum hand?"

Peyton laughed. "I can always type with one finger—like I used to before I learned to keyboard."

Mr. Ford paced the floor, muttering to himself. He swung around and pointed to his computer. "I'm assigning you to my office for a few weeks. Use your skills and discover new avenues for the sale of wool. I sell to the coop in San Angelo, but this year, the amount of money I'll make isn't going to cut it."

Peyton's pulse pounded in his chest. "I can do that.

I'll try my best to help get the ranch in the black."

Mr. Ford clasped Peyton's uninjured hand and shook it. "Honestly, I feel guilty about paying a business specialist a ranch hand's wage, but son, I can't afford to give you a raise."

"I'm not concerned about that. Shall I get to work now?"

Peyton popped the pain pill, took a gulp from his water bottle, and then returned to the computer screen. Over a week now in Mr. Ford's office and he'd already set up a marketing website for the ranch—which should've happened a couple of years ago. Next step: contact more buyers.

He perused the emails and opened the third one, Santa Fe Spindle Company in New Mexico. The company he'd emailed last week.

He read aloud. "We've taken a look at your online information and pictures and are interested in purchasing wool for our hand spinners and weavers. Can you send us a core sample? If the quality meets our needs, we'd like to place a large order. We prefer to work with individual ranchers rather than a co-op."

Peyton gave a thumbs up. "All right." Mr. Ford would be happy to hear about this positive start. He chuckled to himself. Three months ago, he didn't know what a core sample was. Now he did—a sampling from a bale of wool to determine the quality of the fabric. He grinned. Guess that was better than sending an entire sheep to a potential client.

Thirty minutes later, the ranch owner made his way into the office. "How's it going?"

"Do you know where we can get a core sample made?"

Mr. Ford rubbed his hands together. "You bet I do. There's a lab in San Angelo. Though we haven't used them, some of the ranchers I've spoken with say they're reputable."

"We need to send a sample to a company in New Mexico. If the quality is what they're looking for, the corporation will be ready to place a substantial order." Though Peyton was confident he could turn the ranch's finances around, getting approval for some of these steps became imperative. "Sir, I have another idea I want to pass on to you."

"Shoot." Mr. Ford sank into the chair Peyton had occupied a week ago at the meeting.

"Have you considered attending a trade show to secure orders?" Peyton cleared his throat. Though he was doing his job, for some reason making suggestions to Mr. Ford felt intimidating. "There's a large one coming up in Las Vegas soon. You can speak to potential buyers face to face."

He scratched his head. "Las Vegas? I'll give that option some thought."

Peyton turned his focus to the computer. "Your new website is getting attention. We have several companies who want to make small purchases."

The boss nodded. "I've known for a while that I needed to update my marketing efforts. You're an answer to prayer."

Peyton's neck grew warm. Being Mr. Ford's answer to prayer wasn't a bad thing.

"May I ask a personal question?" Mr. Ford said.

Peyton stiffened his shoulders, causing his ribs to ache. He had an inkling of what Mr. Ford might ask—and he couldn't answer. Not now anyway. "Sir, if it's about—"

"Your past. Yes. I can see you aren't ready to talk about that. But there's something I'd like to discuss. My daughter."

"Sir?" Did he believe Peyton wanted to start up a relationship with her? Did Mr. Ford intend to warn him away?

Mr. Ford removed his hat. "You're a fine young man. I'd like to ask you a favor."

"Yes, sir. Anything."

"Erika has always been adventuresome and independent. She's not afraid to take on any job on the ranch." Mr. Ford lowered his voice. "I worry about her. She's a bit impulsive. If I'm not around, can you please keep an eye on her—especially if she's getting herself into something she can't handle."

Peyton nodded, glad the man couldn't hear his thoughts. In Peyton's opinion, Mr. Ford was an overprotective father. Erika was an adult and not a child. She could make decisions on her own. "I'll be happy to watch out for her." But what was the source of the man's fears? And too, Mr. Ford had allowed the question about Peyton's past to slide this time, but someday he'd compel Peyton to reveal what happened.

Chapter Eleven

Two weeks later, Peyton rubbed his hands together, grateful for the progress on the marketing front.

The door opened to Mr. Ford's office, and his boss walked in.

"Just the man I wanted to see. Santa Fe Spindle received the core sample, and the company is ready to place an order. Unfortunately, it's not as large as they'd originally planned."

Though Mr. Ford might be disappointed, Peyton figured the man trusted him—and he didn't want to let him down. "What do you think about selling sheep for milk and meat? I've discovered a few options in that market. Two companies in San Angelo and three in Dallas."

Mr. Ford peered at him. "I've always focused on wool production."

Peyton drew in a long breath, not concerned about confronting the man at this point. "Could be the time has come for you to expand your product to meat or milk, or perhaps both."

Mr. Ford paced the office. "No. Not now. The timing isn't right. The ranch isn't set up for milk production, nor do we raise the appropriate breeds for meat production." He scrubbed a hand over his mouth. "Peyton, I'm depending on you for this."

"Yes, and I don't want to let you down, but it's been over three weeks since the accident. Is it time for me to learn how to shear?" Afterall, Peyton was hired to do physical work on the ranch.

His boss pinched his lips together. "Look, I need for you to continue doing what you're doing—making sales."

When Peyton applied to work as a ranch hand, he never would've believed he'd end up in an office again doing the work he'd left before he went to Peru. "You're the boss. I'll try my best."

Peyton's stomach bottled up inside. The success of Mr. Ford's lifelong calling depended a great deal on Peyton's ability to get the ranch out of the red. But could he?

Peyton pulled the bandage from his hand and tossed the gauze into the garbage in the bunkhouse's bathroom. He showered, dried off with his towel, and donned the t-shirt and warmups he wore to bed. Since he hopefully didn't need the box of cotton dressings anymore, he shoved it into the cabinet drawer.

With only a slight amount of pain in his ribs, he walked from the bathroom into the large bunkroom.

Glasses hooked on his nose, Mac sat up in his bed reading a book.

Peyton eyed his roommate's reading material. As he

figured, the Bible. "You like that book, too?"

Mac peered past his glasses and smiled. "Yep. Been dependin' on the Good Book for many years."

Peyton couldn't restrain the grin. "It's one of my favorites, too."

"I figured as much." Mac glanced at his Bible and to Peyton again. "One time He literally saved my life. I been reading this here book ever since." He lifted up the Bible.

Saved his life? Peyton swallowed hard and asked the question on his mind. "What happened?"

Mac pulled off his glasses and laid them on the bed beside him. "I had a job in Montana on a ranch." Mac cleared his throat. "One day I was working a piece of land with the tractor. I came a little too close to a ditch that I didn't see. The tractor rolled over on me, and I got pinned under. The pain was awful."

Peyton shuddered, reminding him of his own accident and the excruciating pain that followed. "Oh, man. That's tough. But you're here now."

Mac stared at the opposite wall as if he didn't hear Peyton's remark. "I couldn't move my leg, and there was no way to get out on my own. I figured I'd die."

Peyton leaned on the edge of Mac's bed. "What about the owner of the ranch?"

"It was early in the morning." Mac's words flowed in monotone. "It'd be hours before I was missed, if then. I had no hope of getting out." Mac rubbed his forehead. "I was real scared and didn't know what to do. And then I got rescued by a little old lady."

"What?" Peyton smiled. Was Mac pulling his leg or was this a true story? "You're kidding."

"Naw, man. An elderly woman, in chunky shoes

and her white hair in a bun, had gone to town to shop, at least that was what she told me. On her way home, she saw the overturned tractor and stopped her car. She said she wasn't sure what called her attention to the field and tractor on its side, but she trudged over the rocky ground in that direction. Then she said she saw me."

"That's an amazing story. You could no longer help yourself, but an old woman came along. How'd she get you out?"

"That little lady returned with EMS. After they pushed the tractor off, they carried me on a gurney to the ambulance. To this day, I can picture her smiling face, as if comforting me as those guys worked."

Peyton stared at Mac. "Wow. Amazing story."

Mac held his hand to the side of his mouth. "Promise you won't think I'm crazy."

Peyton wasn't so sure, but he wouldn't tell Mac. "Sure."

"Looking back, sometimes I almost think she was an angel."

Peyton laughed and reached to slap Mac's shoulder. "I think you need to get some rest, buddy." He shook his head, still chuckling to himself.

Mac stood beside the bed and lifted one foot then the other. "Well, today I've still got both legs and doing great."

Peyton scratched his head. "When I stepped into the shower a little earlier, I felt like the weight of that bulldozer out in the equipment room rested on my shoulders. I've taken on some responsibilities, and if I don't succeed, this ranch could go under." Peyton grimaced. "You remember the financial difficulties Mr.

Ford talked about."

"Yeah."

"But if God can send a little old lady to rescue you from under a tractor, He can save this ranch." Though the future was uncertain, peace warmed his insides.

But like any industry, sheep ranching depended on good management. Would he hear from the Lord and continue to steer the Ford ranch in the right direction?

Chapter Twelve

Erika wiped her brow, the April air warm in the enclosed sheering barn. She examined the combs, cutters, the electric shears, and the hand blades she'd set out on the back shelf—prepped and waiting to go. She whistled for Sam and pointed toward the sheep barn. "Walk up."

Sam raced into the barn and approached the flock from behind, prompting the lead sheep to move forward. The others followed, jumping and baaing like today was their birthday.

After the last sheep left the barn for the holding pen, chatter from outside indicated the hands were about ready to begin.

Jace, Austin, and Chet strolled through the front door of the sheering barn, the heels of their boots crunching across the packed gravel and straw.

Dad, in some kind of animated conversation, walked toward the shearing area with Mac.

Erika took long strides toward the holding pen. She gazed toward the cloudless sky, her heart drumming in her chest. She'd watched her brothers do the actual work lots of times, and today she determined to give it a try. Get the sheep in position and then shear the animal.

First the belly, then the hind legs, and the chest, neck, and chin.

In the barn, Sam circled the group, barking and nudging the stragglers forward.

After the last sheep loped into the pen, she locked the latch. The twenty-five ewes crowded each other within the enclosure, ears back, a signal they enjoyed the fresh air.

She shook her finger at them. "How hard could it be to take a little wool off you guys? You'll behave, right?" She snickered to herself. "The first bunch is ready to go," she called to the others.

Twenty minutes later, Dad waved from the sheering shed, his indication that they were about to start.

Again, she signaled for Sam to drive the sheep from the pen into the shearing shed. All loped through the barn door except for two stubborn creatures. They baaed and shuffled toward the gate but refused to exit.

In the shearing shed, with Sam's help, the hands coaxed the ewes into smaller enclosures lining the walls. Jace and Austin waited, electric shears in hand. Chet and Mac stood at the table in back attaching blades to their clippers.

Erika paused at the holding pen. "Come here, you two obstinate sheep."

Sam scampered closer and rushed the two from behind. Both ewes moved toward the shearing shed and then backed away.

What was scaring these girls? Did they know what was ahead? Erika shook her head. No, sheep were dumb animals.

She edged closer to the shed's door and took a few steps inside. Puddles from last night's rain had pooled on the floor. The dark, wet spots scared the creatures, as if the water was a black hole. Erika blew out her frustration in a long breath. The animals avoided wet and dark spaces at all costs, and these two were extra dubious.

She picked up a feed bucket and returned to the holding area. Backing out the gate into the shed, she rattled the contents. Both sheep huddled together in the opposite corner, not interested in the offer of food.

"Okay, you asked for it." She held the first sheep against the corral's fence and straddled its rump. Putting one hand on the rail, she placed the other under the sheep's neck like her father had shown her. Using the fence for support, she pulled the sheep onto its hind legs to walk it forward. The sheep slipped from her hand and scampered away. She ground her teeth. Maybe she'd give up and ask Jace to help her. She turned, ready to call her brother.

Then the vision of the ribbons and other awards that she'd won through 4H drifted into her memory. She'd shown sheep at the local fair in Oakville every year growing up, some of the best occasions of her childhood. A couple of times, she'd almost given up on the projects, especially the time when she hadn't properly secured a lamb to bathe him. He'd jumped off the table, injuring himself in the process. But her 4H officer reminded her that if she failed in her efforts, she needed to persist and try again.

"Okay, that's it." Erika gritted her teeth and ran after the stubborn sheep who now cowered near the opposite fence. Tackling the animal once again, she used all the strength she had and walked the animal into the shearing shed.

Jace glanced up. "Thanks, Erika."

"The last one will be here in a minute." Now more than determined than ever, she put the last sheep in a head hold and marched her into the shearing area.

Peyton sauntered around the edge of the barn toward her. "How's it going, Erika?"

She faced him, shoulders back and chin high. "Had to wrangle a few sheep. Nothing out of the ordinary." She chuckled to herself. Mustering up the determination to manhandle those animals had paid off. Especially since Peyton had witnessed what happened. She smoothed down the front of her shirt and smiled at him.

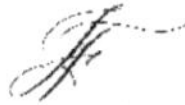

"Good job, Erika. You showed that sheep who's boss." Peyton laughed and rested his arms on the wooden structure forming the sheep's enclosure. Erika's strength and her determination not to give up impressed him. Her smile said she enjoyed the satisfaction of doing her job well. But if he were honest, he'd hope that her grin meant even more. Perhaps that she was glad to see him.

He shook his head. He didn't need to think about Erika in that way. He'd come to the Ford ranch to regroup, to find direction for the rest of his life, a life free of the pain of losing Sandra.

Peyton headed to the main house. Lunch would be served anytime now. Afterward, he'd need to saddle Jack and head out for the north pasture. Being back to physical labor was good after all the time lost due to his fall.

That afternoon, Peyton shifted in his saddle, relieving a bit of discomfort to his ribs. The first time on a horse in more than a month wasn't as painful as he'd expected.

Mac turned in his saddle as they approached the sheep pen. "Glad to see you're on the mend."

"Yeah, me too. Mr. Ford decided I should work half a day in the office and spend the rest of the time doing ranch work. Rounding up a flock of sheep and herding them back to the ranch for shearing is a first for me. But I'm gonna be a genuine ranch hand one of these days."

The flock baaed and loped across the grass and into the sheep enclosure as he and Mac rode behind.

Sam raced around the flock, steering the stragglers through the gate.

Ewe after ewe trotted in, lambs staying close to their mothers. The last ewe, baaing loudly and hesitant to pass through, had black ear tips and spots across her nose. No doubt it was Sadie. But where was her lamb?

Peyton spurred Jack and caught up with Mac. "How often do babies stray from their mothers in the pasture? I see Sadie but not her lamb."

Mac dismounted and closed the pen's gate. "It happens fairly frequently. The offspring can get separated from their mothers. Sometimes a loud noise can spook the creatures and frighten them away from the flock. Last year, I spotted a lamb that decided to explore the terrain. Naturally, a few others followed."

"I'm pretty sure Sadie's isn't here." Peyton got off

Jack and tied him to the post. "None of the lambs have the markings Sadie's has."

"Unless Mr. Ford has you shearing this afternoon, I'd say you've got some free time to go back and search. I'd go with you, but I need to inspect the combs and other tools to make sure they're in good condition."

"Search for what?" Erika strolled toward them from the shearing barn.

"Sadie's lamb. Mac and I think he could still be up in the pasture, vulnerable to predators. I'm going back to look for it. Wanta go?" If he could do anything this afternoon, he'd want to ride with Erika up to the pasture. He smiled.

"Sure. Let's take the truck." She headed to the ranch pickup parked by the barn.

Peyton glanced at Jack where he'd tied him earlier. "Not the horses?"

"We'll need a lasso and a cage to bring him to the ranch. He's not too fond of riding on the back of the horse." She chuckled.

Peyton laughed. "Sounds like you've got experience rescuing lambs."

"Yep, a bit." She grinned, an expression that hinted she enjoyed sharing her knowledge of ranching.

Peyton helped her lift the cage and place the rope in the cargo bed of the pickup.

"I'll drive." She sat in the driver's seat.

Fine with him. Erika was a good teacher.

A mesquite tree scraped the side of the truck as the vehicle bounced on the dirt road. Billows of dust floated into the air. A few more miles and the north pasture appeared with its green grass for grazing.

Erika slowed and then stopped. Pulling out a pair of

binoculars from under the seat, she gazed around the terrain.

Peyton glanced in the opposite direction. "Mac said sometimes a loud noise can scare a lamb away from his mama. Maybe a plane going over or a gun shot?"

"I've seen it happen before." She passed him the binoculars.

"Sadie baaed louder as if overly stressed when she came through the gate." He lifted the binoculars to his eyes. "As if she knew something was wrong."

"Yes. The mama sheep missed her lamb." Erika drove forward fifty more yards. Coyote Creek was visible to the right.

Movement under the oak beside the stream became clearer as he glanced through the binoculars again. "Drive over there by the creek."

Under the tree, a lamb pranced one way and then the other.

"There he is." Peyton pointed to the stream's bank. "See the ear tips and freckles over the nose?"

"What?" She laughed.

"The lamb's markings are the same as Sadie's. I noticed the first day we met in the barn."

A slow smile covered her lips. "I remember the day." Erika cut the motor and exited the truck.

Peyton pulled the cage from the back of the pickup and set it on the ground. He crept toward the creature, Erika by his side.

Erika handed Peyton the rope. "Drop the loop over his head and tightened the knot enough so the lamb won't slip out."

The high-pitched cry told him the creature was hungry. He continued on toward Sadie's offspring, glad

Erika gave him a chance to practice *the art* of going after stray sheep.

The lamb nosed around the grass as if looking for something to eat.

Without a hitch, Peyton eased the loop around its neck and gently urged him toward the truck and into the cage. "You may not like this ride, but we're taking you to see your mama again."

Back in the truck, Erika smiled as she turned the key in the lock. "You're a pro now."

"Ha." Peyton smirked. "Still got a lot to learn about ranching."

For an instant, he wished he could do something about the pitiful wails from the back of the truck. But they only had the animal's best interests in mind.

Erika glanced at him and back to the road. "You look worried."

Peyton laughed at himself. "I confess, I'm taking this sheep business to heart."

She gave a knowing grin. "I understand what you're saying. Caring for the sheep evokes a feeling of compassion, but we need to remember they all aren't going to thrive, and they aren't pets. As a kid, it was hard for me, too."

Erika braked as she pulled up in front of the sheep pen. She jumped out and headed toward the cage. "Here you are, little fellow. Your mama is ready to feed you."

Peyton rushed around to the truck's cargo bed. "Let me." He lifted the cage and set lamb and cage on the grass as Erika opened the gate.

Sadie baaed as her baby ran toward her and began to nurse the minute he arrived.

Erika sidled up to Peyton and gave him a high-five.

"You're turning out to be a mighty fine cowboy."

A strand of her hair brushed against his neck. The aroma of fresh peaches met his nose, fresh even after wrangling with sheep all day.

Electricity traveled from his chest to his stomach. A sensation he hadn't felt in a long time. Not since … Was it too soon to fall for someone again?

That evening Peyton finished the piece of chocolate cake and ran a napkin across his lips.

Mr. Ford rose from his spot at the main table. "As you all know, we support our local group home for disadvantaged boys. I want to remind each of you about the annual bar-b-que coming up this Sunday. I posted a list of duties in my office for everyone. We're hoping to raise more funds than last year. "

Chet fixed his gaze on his hands in his lap, perhaps aware that the money maker supported kids like him.

Peyton's insides warmed. The bar-b-que was the perfect opportunity to learn more about helping needy children and teens. He walked out the front door and around the side of the house toward Mr. Ford's office. Inside the office, the assignment sheet was penned on the bulletin board attached to the wall nearest the exit door.

Mr. Ford strolled into the office from the dining room. "Think you can set up chairs and tables the day of the event?" He settled into his office chair.

"Yes. I lifted a heavy cage this morning without pain. I'm sure I can handle it." He squared his shoulders. "Tell me more about the group home."

Mr. Ford thumbed through a stack of papers and then glanced at him. "Oakville established the community home about fifteen years ago and serves boys without a stable place to live. They also take kids where both parents are absent from their lives. The home services the entire region of central Texas from as far south as San Antonio and Waco to the north."

"If I might ask, why the special interest in needy boys?" He could ask himself the same.

"Fair question. Back in grade school, I used to know a kid whose mother died of drug overdose. He lived with his alcoholic father." Mr. Ford stared out the glass window. "Sometimes that boy was home alone for days at a time. Filthy, smelly. The other kids used to make fun of him, but his circumstances touched my heart. Mom and Dad had him out to the ranch a couple of times. His face always lit up when he had dinner with my family. I could see the hunger in those hurting eyes."

"What happened to him?"

"Fortunately, his father's mother came to take him home with her to Arizona. Last I heard, he was doing well. A college graduate with a wife and several kids, now mostly grown. That's the kind of results I want to see for any needy boy." Mr. Ford strolled around the room. "I'll never forget that kid and how he relished visiting the ranch. My wife and I began the fundraisers about ten years ago for the home in Oakville."

Peyton faced Mr. Ford. "I have a similar dream. To run a ranch for wayward boys. A ranch where boys have room to roam, do ranching chores, and live with a housemother and housefather. A place with a country atmosphere."

Mr. Ford pushed his glasses up on his nose. "I like the notion. Your ranch would be a second option to the home in Oakville. Social services would have a choice as to where to place kids." He slapped Peyton on the back. "Proud of you, son." Mr. Ford's touch sent warmth to Peyton's heart.

He started out the door but stopped. Then Peyton stiffened his shoulders where only moments ago he'd enjoyed reassurance from the rancher's touch. Peyton could run the ranch serving as a housefather, but what about a housemother? He'd lost his wife in the jungles of Peru, never to return.

"You okay, Peyton?" Mr. Ford asked.

Peyton nodded without turning. "Yes, sir."

His dream had died just as quickly as it had been born.

Chapter Thirteen

Rows of cars and vans filled the parking area between Austin's place and the side of Jace and Charlotte's house. More than last year, Erika guessed.

In the middle of the front yard, Austin had a stick horse in hand and was surrounded by a group of kids.

Erika covered her smile. Wouldn't do for her brother, Austin, to see her laughing at him at the annual bar-b-que. Even so, she couldn't help giggling as she watched his demonstration.

He blew a whistle, and kids straddled their broom handle horses, a chorus of bystanders cheering them on. A boy about nine came up from behind and loped across the finish line ahead the others. Again, the small crowd cheered, as if the contestant had won the Kentucky Derby.

She shaded her eyes with one hand and gazed across the wide area in front of their ranch style home. More activities than last year were set up around the ranch.

Erika passed the main house in the direction of the bunkhouse. She smiled at Mom as she sat at a table, painting on little faces to make the kids look like sheep and horses.

The petting zoo sat beyond Peyton's quarters to the west. Erika checked the schedule on her phone. Time for her shift to supervise and give Jace and Charlotte a break.

About five boys stood next to the makeshift wire cage with the lambs poking their noses through. A small boy of about six stuck his index finger in and giggled as a lamb nudged him with his nose.

Charlotte nodded at Erika. "Now that you're finally here, I've got to finish setting up the serving tables."

Erika forced a smile at her already cantankerous sister-in-law. "You bet. Yours and Mom's bar-b-que dinner is the biggest moneymaker." One day, they'd be friends, she hoped.

Behind her about fifteen feet, a boy of probably twelve or thirteen, leaned against the gigantic oak tree she used to climb as a kid. With shoulders slumped forward, he eyed the other kids with a look that Erika would guess meant deep loneliness—maybe even rejection. Erika shrugged. Perhaps he thought he was too old to enjoy the activity.

She motioned to him. "Come on over and take a look at these lambs. A few of them are only a week old." She pointed to the fuzzy creature nearest the fence. "We may have to take her to her mama pretty soon."

He ducked his head and stared at the freshly cut grass growing under the oak.

Poor kid, he needed a bit of coaxing. Erika took a few cautious steps toward him. "That's fine if you want to look at the lambs from where you're standing. What's your name?"

He diverted his gaze to his feet, as if avoiding eye

contact and mumbled something unintelligible.

Erika's heart broke for the kid. The timid boy probably didn't think he was welcome. She arrived at his side and pointed toward the lambs. "Do you suppose you could help me name them? It's a big job."

He rubbed the back of his neck as he walked toward the cage. "Okay." He neared the lamb closest to the wire. "That one's name could be Henry."

Erika grinned. "Great name. Is Henry a special name to you?"

The boy looked past her shoulder as if remembering another time and place. "Back when I lived at home, I had a friend named Henry. I haven't seen him since I er, moved."

"Henry it is." Home meaning before he was taken to live in the group home. The memory must've been painful. "We'll remember Henry by the markings on his nose. He looks like he was digging in a dirt pile with his face. See that big splotch?"

"Yep." The boy put his finger through the fence and chuckled when one of the lambs rubbed his head on his hand. "That one should be called Pal because he's so friendly."

"I like that. You're pretty good at this." Anything to boost the boy's outlook.

He rubbed the back of his neck and red splotches appeared on his cheeks.

She dared a question. "How long have you lived in the Oakville home?"

He shook his head and turned to walk back to the tree.

Erika patted his shoulder. "Hey, I'm sorry I asked a nosy question. I didn't mean to make you uncomfortable."

"Nah, that's okay." He shrugged and continued toward the tree. "I don't feel like talking no more."

As many years as Erika had worked the bar-b-que, she'd never seen a kid as withdrawn as this boy. "I don't blame you. I feel that way sometimes." Not just a statement to uplift him, but the truth.

He leaned against the tree again, this time his heel resting on the trunk. "I used not to be like that … "

Erika wouldn't have guessed he'd open up with a response at that moment. But the boy's words brought her hope she could help him. He merely needed someone to listen. "Oh?" Since her last question hadn't helped, she gazed at him waiting to see what else he'd say. Hopefully he'd open up on his own again.

"I used to talk a lot to my brother."

She wanted to ask about his brother but wouldn't. He'd close up like the locked door of the bank vault in Oakville.

A sense of heaviness settled in her heart. The young teen had not always lived in a boys' home. He'd had a family once, but what happened? Erika turned to the sound of footsteps.

Chet passed the bunkhouse and meandered toward the petting zoo. "Hey, Erika. Your dad is getting ready to give the kids a safety demonstration about what to do in case of fire. Stop, drop, and roll. He sent me to check if there are any kids over here who want to come."

"Sure." She glanced around the area. Two children about eight and nine still stood near the lamb cages. She looked at the shy kid. "Maybe this guy would like to go."

Chet glanced at the boy. Then as if he'd seen a dead

person, he froze. After a few seconds, he blew out a quick breath. "I don't believe it." With wide eyes, he stared toward the tree where the boy leaned.

Erika walked closer to Chet. "What is it?" She'd never seen Chet display those kinds of emotions.

A hesitant smile crossed his face, and he raced toward the oak, his boots clunking on the ground.

"Chet, what's going on?" She wrinkled her brow.

Chet brushed a tear from his cheek as he threw his arms around the boy. "I can't believe you're here."

Dad hadn't shared much background information about Chet, but Chet obviously knew the boy. She neared Chet and placed her hand on his shoulder. "Is everything okay?"

He slowly turned to her, his eyes bright with tears. "This here's my brother, Pete."

Peyton shook Grandpa Martin's hand and headed toward the tool shed. The last time he checked the computer, online donations were greater than last year. From what Mr. Ford told him, local attendees would make donations when they paid for their meal. To think, one rancher paid one thousand dollars last year for a meal of brisket, coleslaw, baked beans, bread, and apple pie. And if Charlotte and Mrs. Ford were preparing the food, the supper would be delicious.

Mac sat on a folding chair next to the shed with a book in his hand and surrounded by five kids. "Jonah was in the belly of that whale for three days and three nights. Then the big creature vomited Jonah up on dry land."

"Eww." The kids wrinkled their noses.

"But after that, God was able to use Jonah in His work."

Peyton snickered at the sight of the big, burly ranch hand reading to small children. He headed toward the other side of the house to the petting zoo to relieve Erika.

Rounding the corner past the sheep shearing barn and the bunk house, he spotted the pens set up to house the lambs.

Voices to the right under the giant oak next to the main house's yard caught his attention.

Chet had his arm around one of the kids as they talked with Erika.

Peyton caught his breath. The kid looked a lot like Chet. Was the boy …? He caught up to the group and glanced at Erika.

She smiled and nodded as if she'd read his mind.

"Chet?" Peyton said.

The young ranch hand turned around with a smile as wide as the north pasture. "It's Pete. He lives at the place in Oakville. The state sent him to foster care about six months ago." He stopped to catch his breath. "To think, I showed up here after that. That's fate for you."

"No, buddy." Peyton smiled and patted Chet's shoulder. "That's got to be the doings of the Lord."

Chet stared at him. "You think God would do something like that for me and my brother?"

Peyton nodded. "You bet. I know He would." He approached the kid who had the same curly hair and blue eyes as Chet. "Nice to meet you, Pete. I hope you can come see us again since you two guys live so close." He'd make sure that would happen. "Chet talks about you a lot."

Pete shrugged. "Yeah. As long as he don't tell no stories about me." A grin hinted that he spoke in jest.

Erika stood wide eyed as she undeniably took in the scene before her.

Peyton grasped both boys by their shoulders. "I promise you guys, I'll do everything I can to keep you together from now on."

Erika switched on her flashlight and made one last sweep around the area that only hours ago was alive with giggling children running to each activity and where grownups had devoured spicy barbeque at the long tables near the house. The pens were quiet after Austin and Peyton had returned the lambs to their mothers. Another successful fundraiser.

"Hey." The familiar voice drawled behind her.

Peyton's frame became visible as she shined the flashlight in his direction. "Hey, yourself."

"I jumped in the shower to get some of the smokey bar-b-que odor off me. Now I need to check on the sheep." With no Stetson propped on his head, his spikey, dark strands looked wet.

Before she thought about it, she stood next to him and sniffed his jaw. The scent of sandalwood enticed her to draw closer. "Umm. You smell nice." She took another deep breath, her nose only a half inch from his cheek. "Like the aroma of a rainforest."

Peyton's deep voice rumbled in her ear. "I figured the sheep would approve." His laugh at his own joke was contagious, and she snickered, too.

Did his aftershave contain some exotic ingredient? She tried to ignore her racing heart. She wanted to cozy up to him and absorb the scent. But she couldn't get interested in this guy. She knew nothing about him or what happened in his mysterious past. Yet she couldn't deny that standing close made her lightheaded. She never would've imagined that a gorgeous wrangler would show up at the Ford's ranch—a guy who caused her to dream of a life with him someday. She stepped two strides away.

"Wanta walk with me to the sheep barn to check on the ewes and lambs?" Peyton took a few slow paces in that direction.

Though she should say no, she didn't. "Sure." The lambs. The thought brought back memories of this afternoon at the petting pens and Chet's brother. "That was an amazing coincidence today when Chet met up with his brother Pete. What were the chances?"

In the moonlight, she could see Peyton's square jawline and his enchanting smile.

He searched her face. "It was no coincidence those brothers met as they did today."

No coincidence? Erika nodded yet she supposed Peyton would tell her God was responsible—well, maybe so.

At the door to the barn, Peyton turned to face her. His gaze seemed to be fixed on her lips. "Erika, I ... " He leaned an inch toward her, his eyes bright with anticipation.

The ewes baaed and bleated to each other, as if to

say "Come on into our house."

Was he planning to kiss her?

As if Peyton woke from a dream, he took a few steps back as he cleared his throat. He raked a nervous hand through his dark hair. "Guess I better check the animals before it gets too late."

Erika laughed. "We don't want to keep them up past their bedtime."

Peyton's beam said he smiled for her only. He lit up her life, and she wanted to be nowhere else.

The melodious song of the mockingbird added a background of music.

Peyton's warm hand covered hers, and he whispered. "You've brought me hope again."

Again? What happened in the past that had stolen his hopes—his dreams from him?

Chapter Fourteen

Peyton poured a second cup of steaming coffee into his mug from the carafe on the side table. He strolled out the front door into the glorious summer day. A choir of early morning birds chirped a tune. He couldn't help puckering up and whistling along.

The flower garden in front of the ranch house was bright with chrysanthemums, geraniums, and lilies—more colorful than usual.

Last night had surprised him. He never expected to almost kiss Erika. If he'd followed his instincts, he would've captured her lips with his, but she might not feel the same about him. More than that, he surprised himself by discovering he had feelings for her. He'd never have predicted those emotions would return to his life.

Why was he so aware of the sweet aromas from the gardenias growing in the flowerbed around the Ford's estate? He palmed his forehead. *Face it, Langston. You're falling in love.* Was now the time and was Erika the right girl?

Erika strolled into the den, the news blaring from the seventy-inch TV. Yesterday, working the petting zoo, the kitchen cleanup, and making sure every child was on the bus exhausted her. Besides, she hadn't slept well last night, thoughts of Peyton's beautiful face in the moonlight captivating her thoughts.

Mac, Peyton, Austin, Chet, and Dad relaxed on the couch and the easy chairs. Austin hiked one leg over the side of his seat, and Mac crossed his feet at his ankles, legs extended on the floor. Peyton folded his arms over his chest, eyes half closed. No doubt the guys were as bushed as she.

She plopped down on the couch next to Dad, his feet propped up on the coffee table.

He patted her hand. "We made more money for the boys' home this year than ever before."

"That's wonderful, Dad. Everyone's efforts were all worth it."

Dad's eyes twinkled. "I'd like to start a college fund for one or two of the boys who'll graduate high school in a couple of years. There're likely some who'll want to attend the university in Lubbock or even the University of Texas."

Erika laced her fingers behind her head. "A wise use of the money, in my opinion. I guess you heard about Chet finding his little brother, Pete."

Chet glanced toward them, a wide grin on his face. "One of the best days of my life. We're together again—like a family."

Dad nodded at Chet. "We're hoping to have Pete out to the ranch for frequent visits."

Peyton looked from the TV to her and Dad. "Chet's

going to be happy about that."

"Hey. You talking about me, too?" Chet smiled again.

"Yep. And I volunteer to go into town to pick up Pete." Peyton said.

A scene flashed on the screen of a riot in a large northeastern city. One man, a hoodie disguising his face, hurled a tear gas canister through the window of a local market. A fire flamed in the grocery store and the building next door. Others, their faces concealed by masks, screamed obscenities not more than a foot away from police officers' faces. Gun shots fired in the background.

Erika caught her breath as she faced the truth. Violence filled her country—a departure from the morality of her childhood days. Yet the ranch seemed a haven from the devastation at times.

Peyton sprang from his chair and headed to the front door, his movements more abrupt than she would've expected on the quiet evening. He held his fists in tight balls, breathing hard, and then walked out onto the porch.

Strange he hadn't said goodnight. Something must have bothered him. The news? After ten minutes, Erika stood and looked out the front window. No Peyton. Perhaps he'd gone to bed. She turned toward the den in the back of the house, and glanced out the rear windows.

Visible in the moonlight, Peyton sat in the swing at the edge of the yard, swaying back and forth.

On impulse, Erika set out across the grass toward him. "Hey. Anyone sitting here?"

He scooted over and shrugged. "If you want."

Elbow resting on his knee, he held his head, eyes closed, and rubbed his temple with a circular motion of his shaking hand.

Undoubtedly, he had a headache, but she decided to give the guy some space. He'd speak when he was ready.

For more than five minutes, they sat in silence with only the night creatures uttering their usual chirps and hoots. The evening air brought the scent of rose bushes from the side garden.

Peyton's breath came in sharp spurts, finally slowing to normal.

Erika restrained the urge to touch his arm. Still, she waited, not sure if he'd want to open up or not. After five more minutes, she braved the question. "What's going on, Peyton?"

He jammed his hands into his armpits. "Nothing."

Erika chuckled to herself. A typical answer for a guy. She wouldn't let him get away with that response. "Doesn't seem like nothing. You left so suddenly."

He coughed into his fist and stared straight ahead. "I don't like hearing about riots and violence."

What? Was he one of those people who stuck his head in the sand and avoided unpleasant situations. If she'd guessed correctly, there had to be another reason he abruptly left the family room. "I suppose no one does."

They sat in silence again.

"The violence, the screams and angry words, the gun shots." Peyton's words were soft, filled with tension, as if he didn't like what he was to say.

She held her breath to hear him.

"Another time and place, conflict and violence ... "

He swept his hand through his hair. "Best I don't I talk about it now."

"I didn't mean to make you uncomfortable." Something awful must've happened in the past. He reminded her of a soldier who'd suffered PTSD. Her heart melted like soft butter. If holding him in her arms would help, she'd do it.

Peyton swallowed the turbulence filling his throat and threatening to uproot his composure. Watching the riots on the news—he couldn't take anymore. The violence launched a panic attack, initiating memories from the past. An episode perhaps worse than the others bullied him. The heat from Erika's warm body next to him did nothing to calm the anxiety in his soul. He gulped.

Erika's smooth hand brushed over his shoulder. "Are you okay. My female intuition tells me differently."

He rested his elbows on his knees again, covering his face with his hands. "Something on the TV. Reminded me of the past." A past that he'd done everything possible to flee from.

He turned to gaze into her eyes. Did he dare tell her about those days in Peru? If he opened up, the recollections would only bring to life again the terror and his failure to save Sandra. He coughed, barely able to breathe. No, he couldn't speak of it now.

"Shh. It's okay." Erika whispered.

"Violence, greed, resistance, I've seen it, been

there."

Erika smoothed her hand over his. "Try to relax. We can talk about this another time."

He nodded. "Yes, another time." But how could he overcome the flashbacks, the anxiety, the regret?

Chapter Fifteen

Peyton squirmed as he shifted from side to side on the passenger seat. He took a deep breath in an attempt to decompress. No doubt, yesterday's news report of riots and violence in the northeast triggered the flashback, bringing on another panic attack. He had to heal—let the past go if he expected to lead a normal life again. How many times would he have to tell himself that what happened was not his fault? And that there was nothing he could've done.

In the driver's seat, Jace pressed the gas pedal and headed for the south pasture. "I suppose you know all about mending these fences, but let's not repeat the mistake you made last time. I'm not sure why Dad assigned you to go with me today."

Gritting his teeth, Peyton pressed his lips together. The dig was meant to affirm that Jace was in charge, and Peyton better understand his authority. Which was fine. He wasn't after Jace's job or his place in the family.

The fence line Peyton and Erika had inspected when he first arrived came into view.

Jace raced the truck faster on the makeshift road jostling Peyton up and down in the vehicle's cab. The truck's ceiling whacked Peyton's head as they maneuvered over a pothole. "Hey, buddy, you want to slow down a little?"

Jace glared toward him and increased the speed. "You telling me what to do? I'm the owner's son. I been working this ranch for a long time." Jace's face turned red. "You need to keep your complaints to yourself."

Peyton lifted his palms. "Look, Jace. I don't know what's eating at you. Do you have something against me?"

Jace pulled up a few feet in front of a fence where time and weather had rusted the wire and eroded the posts. He gripped the steering wheel hard. "For one thing, you act like a better-than-thou phony. You think you're going to get in good with my dad by attending his church."

Peyton's mouth dropped open. He didn't care one bit for that last comment. "My faith has nothing to do with your parents. I'm not trying to get in good with your father—or anybody else. Peyton bit down on something gritty, probably the fine dirt that filtered into the truck.

Jace pushed open the door and got halfway out. "You think you're going to earn Dad's favor, marry my sister, and take over? I'm here to tell you there's no way you're getting by with that. This ranch will always stay in the hands of a Ford, you can be sure of that."

Peyton threw up his hands, his jaws aching from clenched teeth. "You've got it wrong." He attempted to steady his voice. "That's not my thing. I don't manipulate people like that. I want to do the best job I can around the ranch."

Jace lifted both hands as if to say *stop*. "Yeah, yeah, sure."

If he could make peace with this guy, he would. "Listen, Jace—"

Jace laughed and looked toward the sky. Then he exited the truck like his backside was on fire.

Peyton rubbed his neck. Did Erika's brother actually think Peyton was trying to gain control over the ranch? What had Peyton done to make him think that?

Peyton hauled the fence stretcher, wire cutters, new posts, and the roll of wire from the truck's bed. He stopped a couple of feet behind Jace who inspected the work necessary to repair the broken fence. Good thing Mr. Ford had placed Jace in charge of this job. The fence was more damaged than the one Peyton and Chet had repaired in the north pasture.

"You might as well watch and learn something today. Teaching you how to do this would take more time than it's worth." Jace donned heavy work gloves. Using a shovel, he dug a hole around the bottom and loosened the old post. After removing the rotted one, he cleared out the hole. "Get me that sack of sand in the back of the truck."

Peyton slipped on a pair of work gloves and hauled the bag out of the truck bed, setting it down next to the repair job.

"Okay." Jace added a layer of sand. "Now bring me the new post from the truck."

Peyton did as he was told and lifted the heavy wooden piece on his shoulders.

Jace set the new post in the hole and filled the space with concrete and water.

Sweat rolled off Peyton's forehead, and he swiped the moisture away. He had to hand it to the guy, he knew his way around ranching. But after all, Erika's brother had been raised in the environment.

Finally, he made loops in one end of the wire and tied them to new corner post. He reached toward the ground to pick up the wire cutters. "Ouch." He stood, holding his left hand.

A snake with a copper-colored head and hourglass-shaped stripes slithered away.

Peyton rushed to his side. "Are you okay?"

Jace's eyes were big, and he peeled off his left glove. He rasped. "That thing bit me. Take off that bandana from around your neck and tie it around my wrist."

"Applying a tourniquet isn't a good idea."

"You're crazy." Jace put his mouth on the bite and sucked.

"No. I know a bit about first aid. You shouldn't do that either." He reached in Jace's pocket and got the keys to the truck. "I need to get you to the hospital to be evaluated. A copperhead's bite isn't fatal, but you may need antivenom."

"My hand's swelling." Jace groaned.

"Okay, let's get in the truck. You need to sit down and stay calm. Keep your hand at heart level." Peyton gripped Jace's right arm and sat him the passenger's seat. "I'll see to the equipment later. It's more important I get you to the doctor."

Jace leaned against the seat and breathed hard.

Peyton started the ignition and raced along the road toward the ranch, dust flying in his wake. He fished his cell phone from his pocket and punched Erika's number. When messages came on, he lowered his voice. No sense in adding to Jace's angst. "Erika, I'm on the way to Oakville General. Jace was bitten by a snake. Let your dad know."

Jace groaned. "Hand hurts—" He gasped and held his throat, emitting gurgling sounds.

Peyton slammed on the brakes and dashed to the passenger side. Time wasn't on his side.

"Agh." Jace's face turned crimson.

Grabbing the horse blanket from the truck's bed, Peyton threw it onto the ground. Then he hauled Jace from the passenger seat onto the blanket. He rolled him to his back and opened his airway like he'd learned in class. "Dear God, please help Jace breathe. Help me to get him the help he needs."

Peyton knelt on the dirt road, wringing his hands as he hovered over Jace. "Please, Lord." He reached again to repeat the mouth-to-mouth resuscitation.

Before he started, Jace sucked in a breath and began to breathe normally.

Peyton folded his hands under his chin. "Thank You, God, for taking care of this man." Peyton pulled out his phone again and dialed Mr. Ford's number, which he should've done in the first place. "Sir, Peyton here. Jace is having a reaction to a snake bite and needs an ambulance. Can you send one to the south pasture as soon as possible. I'm afraid to move him."

"Oh, no." Panic laced the man's voice. "I'll call, and I'll be right there."

Peyton continued to kneel beside the man who appeared to be conscious and no long struggled to breathe. "Help is on the way."

Jace blinked a couple of times, staring at Peyton. "Thank you for taking care of me," he muttered.

The next afternoon, Peyton left the barn and glanced toward the voices coming from Jace and Charlotte's house.

Jace rested in a lawn chair on the wide porch that ran across the front, and Charlotte set a glass of something on the side table next to him.

Now would be a good time to talk about his overnight stay at Oakville General.

Jace waved with his good hand.

Peyton shuffled back a few steps. Jace gave him a friendly greeting? Or maybe he was waving him off. Peyton forged forward and took the porch stairs. "How you doing?"

Jace rested his bandaged hand on the side of the chair and motioned to a yard chair beside him. "Sit."

Peyton's chest tightened. Did Jace plan to scold him again?

"I was hoping to talk to you," Jace muttered, and Peyton could barely hear his hushed voice. "Did a lot of thinking in the last twenty-four hours lying up there in that hospital."

But what kind of thoughts? Maybe he came home with more animosity than he'd had at the fence site.

Jace twisted in the chair with a pillow behind his back. "The ER doc prescribed an antivenom because of my reaction. Some people stop breathing as I did. You were correct to tell me not to use a tourniquet."

Peyton slipped into the chair next to Jace. "It's all over now."

Jace dropped his chin to his chest and covered his

eyes with his right hand. "I could've died." He lifted his swollen bandaged hand and looked up. "You saved my life."

Peyton focused on Jace. "I'm glad I could help yesterday."

Jace glanced skyward as if studying the puffy clouds. "Lying in that bed in the ER gave me some time to remember."

"Remember?" Peyton couldn't guess what the guy was referring to.

Jace frowned and fidgeted with the fabric on his shirt. "I've acted like a jerk where you were concerned."

Instead of a rebuke, a confession. Peyton smiled, not wanting to interrupt.

Jace ducked his head. "Wanted to say I'm sorry."

"I appreciate that." Peyton never dreamed he'd hear those words from the boss's son, but sometimes coming to the end of one's self can change a man's heart.

"When you first showed up on the ranch, I was suspicious of you." Jace angled his shoulders away and paused. Then he curved toward Peyton again. "As time went on, I figured you were out to worm your way into my family. To get in good with my dad and marry my sister for her money—and to take over the ranch."

"Why would you think that?"

"Thought a lot about the reasons, too." Jace rubbed his forehead. "If you must know the truth, I think I was envious. The college educated man from the big city of Dallas coming to our ranch." Jace's cheeks reddened. "But I can see now, you only wanted to help Dad get the ranch out of the red. You were willing to muck out the sheep and horse pens without complaining plus a lot of other dirty chores."

"I told you. I left my job in Dallas to work in South America before coming to the ranch. The ranch offered a change from that life—which was my purpose in answering your father's ad for a ranch hand."

"When I was lying in the dirt on that dusty road, I heard you praying for me. Thank you." He ran his hand through his hair. "What kind of job did you have in South America?"

Peyton rubbed his hand across his mouth. Was he ready to reveal the details? No. "My church sent me down there for a while." Peyton stood. "I need to get to work. I'm glad you're okay."

Peyton headed off toward the tool shed. If he answered one question, Jace would ask another. If Peyton revealed the facts of his past to anyone, it would be to Erika. And even then, the memories and the pain would rip his heart out.

Erika frowned and marched toward the bunkhouse. If she had to pound on the door and go in, she would. She couldn't wait another minute to talk to Peyton. For one thing, guilt had punished her since yesterday when she'd missed Peyton's phone call. Motion to her right caught her attention.

Peyton headed to the tool shed.

"Hey, Peyton." She waved.

He paused looking her way as she neared him.

She arrived and stood face to face. "When I visited with Jace in the hospital last night, he said you'd saved his life." She spoke over the heaviness in her lungs. "I can't thank you enough."

Peyton scraped his boot's heel on the grass. "Anyone would've done the same."

"Nevertheless, I'm grateful you were able to care for him until the ambulance came. He's my brother, and I love him despite our differences." She swiped at a tear. "He said you used first aid to revive him. Where'd you learn that?"

"I, er, picked it up after college." He gave her a nervous glance.

She should've expected a vague answer. Understanding snapped into place in her mind. His knowledge of first aid was a part of his past he avoided talking about at all costs. "You're a brave man, Peyton."

Peyton's smile stretched across his face. "I wasn't exactly his favorite person before the incident, but we talked this afternoon. We're on good terms now." He turned toward the toolshed again.

Erika touched his shoulder to delay him. His firm muscle under her fingers sent an electric tingle through her hand. "Another thing. I feel terrible I didn't answer my phone. I left it in the car when I went to the post office to pick up the mail in Oakville."

"Don't beat up on yourself." He leaned closer. "I could've done the same."

His encouragement helped her to let go of some of the regret. "Please don't think me nosey, but what happened between you and Jace." She touched his arm. "Unless it's none of my business."

Peyton grinned and his ears turned red. "He, er, thought I was trying to take over the ranch by coming after you. He said he thought I was trying to marry you."

She held a strand of hair off her face and released it again. "I never expected that Jace would say that."

"He apologized and said he realized he was wrong."

Wasn't that what he was saying? Disappointment settled over her. Somewhere hidden inside, she'd hoped that they might someday fall in love. Now she knew the truth. He had no intention of going after her.

Chapter Sixteen

Peyton looked up from the computer and stared straight ahead at nothing in particular. Every time he'd awakened last night, he'd relived Erika's soft hand on his shoulder. Not since Sandra had a woman caught his attention in that way.

"Morning, Peyton." Mr. Ford walked into the office.

"Good morning, sir. Three more clients this week. God willing, the ranch will be in the black pretty soon."

Mr. Ford slapped Peyton's shoulder. "I've gone over all the books as well. We're not there yet, so we need to keep pushing forward. But Peyton, you've been a God-send."

"Thanks." Standing on firm ground with the boss was a good place to be. "Those are mighty kind words."

Mr. Ford laughed. "Those aren't kind words. They're the truth."

Peyton rose from his seat in front of the computer. "As long as we can continue to identify profitable markets for the sale of wool, we should be fine. I honestly believe the difficulties stem from rising costs in our economy. Let's hope the price of living stabilizes over the next year."

Mr. Ford steepled his hands. "The older I get, the

more I realize how much I depend on others: my family, the hands, now you." Mr. Ford glanced out the window. "I'd like you to continue working a half day in the office, but this afternoon, I need you to take a ride in the ATV around the ranch. Look for any dead sheep and bury them out in the landfill of the west pasture."

"Yes, sir." Not the easiest job.

"And I'd like Erika to go with you."

Peyton stiffened his shoulder muscles. "I prefer that Austin go instead. Is that a problem?"

In the tool shed, Erika offloaded the last bottle of the spray weed killer from the box she'd picked up Tuesday at the UPS store. She tapped her fingers on the worktable. Hadn't Dad ordered the granular product, not this spray?

Picking up the invoice, she headed to the house to check Dad's records. She turned toward the office door and paused as she heard two males talking. Peyton's familiar voice caught her attention.

Dad spoke next. "I'd like Erika to ride with you."

"I prefer that Austin go instead. Is that a problem?"

Her pulse pounded in her chest. Peyton didn't want her to go with him on some job? Was he convinced that Austin could do better? She bit her lip and returned to the tool shed. She'd check the records after lunch when the skeptical ranch hand wasn't around.

As the sun set, Peyton drank in the aroma of leather and the musty smell of horses—a warm and sweet essence. One of his favorite jobs—brushing the animals.

He used the curry comb to loosen the dirt on Jack's coat. Then with the soft body brush, he groomed the horse's chestnut hair until it shone.

The barn's door squeaked as someone pushed it open. Erika's mouth dropped as she spotted him tending to Jack. "Oh, I saw the lights on in here and thought someone had forgotten to turn them off."

He smiled. "No, just me. Jack worked hard today transporting me around the ranch. I figured he needed special attention."

Erika gripped her fist into tight balls. "I see. Well, I hope you and Austin accomplished your chore today." Her eyes blazed, as if she was ready to use him for target practice with her gun. "Did you actually find him more helpful than I?" She whirled around and walked out the door.

Peyton stared at the barn's exit. What was that about? Had he done something to offend her?

He gave Jack another pat and shook his head. "Hey, fellow. I hope you understand your mare friends better than I do this woman."

Chapter Seventeen

Peyton sipped the last of his breakfast coffee and stood. He stared at Erika's empty spot at the main table. Did she skip the meal this morning or maybe she'd eaten earlier? In any case, her message came through loud and clear last night. She was angry about something.

In the hall leading to the back of the house, Erika held an empty plastic basket. She turned in at the laundry room.

He picked up his pace. If he could clear up the misunderstanding, he'd feel a lot happier. He set out down the hall in her direction and stopped at the room with the washers and dryers to peek in. "Hey, Erika. Can we talk?"

She hauled towels from a large, economy-sized drier and shoved the laundry into the basket. She jerked her head toward him.

Instead of anger, he saw something he hadn't expected. Could he be wrong? Her eyes radiated pain. If he'd hurt her, all the more reason to resolve the misunderstanding.

He lifted the basket from her and set it on the floor. "Talk to me. I can't apologize unless you tell me what I did."

"I thought you were different," she sighed.

He frowned. "I have no idea what you mean."

Her expression held an ache, feelings he'd likely placed there. "I overheard you talking to my father." She folded her hands over her chest." You asked for Austin to work with you though he'd assigned me. What did you think Austin could do that I couldn't?"

He tapped his forehead. So that was it. She'd heard him and her father discussing the work assignment. No doubt she thought he didn't believe her capable of a task. He faced her. "Erika, your dad wanted me to inspect the ranch for dead sheep. I know how distasteful the job is for you. I was trying to spare you."

She studied his face another moment, as if allowing his words to sink in, and then she gripped his hand. "I see. You were thinking of me. I'm sorry, Peyton. I should've … "

"Should've what?"

"Should've known you wouldn't refuse to work with me because you thought I couldn't do the job."

He smiled and restrained the desire to pull her close—into his arms. "You're a strong woman. I respect you." He laughed. "You're willing to take a risk, and I admire that quality in you. Remember what I said? There are a lot of things women can do that we men can't."

"Yeah, like what?" She laughed and wrinkled her nose.

"Like becoming a man's wife and giving him a child." The words emerged before he'd thought. Why had he uttered them? Did they reflect his own desire?

A soft flush covered her cheeks. Maybe he'd gone

too far in trying to console her. "I'm sorry, er ..."

"No, it's me who needs to ask for forgiveness. I realize there's a problem I should iron out with my father instead of projecting my doubts onto you."

Peyton leaned against the washing machine as tension lifted from his shoulders. "If you want to talk, I'm a good listener."

"I'll take you up on that." She trusted Peyton. Clearly, he was a good listener, but something else occurred to her, something she hadn't thought about before. She picked up the laundry basket and set it on the folding table. "Can you meet me at the swinging chair in the backyard?"

"You got it." Peyton turned to leave.

Erika folded the laundry and stacked the towels on the shelves. Why had she become uncomfortable when she thought Peyton hadn't trusted her ability to work? She had to accept the fact that she'd become vulnerable where Peyton was concerned. She'd become way too emotional about this handsome guy.

Talking to him would be for the best. Ten minutes later and laundry folded, she joined Peyton on the swing. Erika dropped next to him, their legs touching. She leaned back on the wooden slats and tried to relax her tense muscles.

"Erika, what you tell me today goes no further."

Something she'd expect the guy to say. Warmth spread through her chest, and she smoothed her hand over his large, calloused one resting on his knee.

"You're a good friend." And more, she'd begun to realize.

His wide smile quickened her pulse. "None of us go through life problem-free. We need each other."

Like she needed him. Erika nodded. "Daddy thinks I can't do the job my brothers can—which is difficult when I'm trying to learn the operation of this ranch." She cleared her throat. "I think he's trying to protect me from something."

Peyton pushed the swing with his boot. "As I grew up, my father treated me differently than my sister. He used to sing with her and listen when she talked about her feelings." He laughed. "He was all rough-and-tumble with me."

"I get it, but I'm no longer a child. Another thing, I've noticed he's reluctant to talk about his sister, my aunt. As if he's keeping something from me." She paused to gain control of her annoyance.

"What do you think your dad might be protecting you from?" He started the swing into motion again.

She huffed a breath. "Since I began working on the ranch full time, Dad always says I should go inside and help Mom and Charlotte instead of assigning me a job in the barn or the pasture. He's never spoken the actual words, but I'm sure he thinks women aren't as capable as men."

Peyton winked. "He assigned you to work with me in the north pasture before I asked for Austin."

She lowered her lashes. "You're right. I'm sure he figured out how I feel when a lamb or sheep dies and wanted me to face my problem."

He smiled. "He cares a lot about you." Peyton coaxed a strand of hair off her neck, his fingers caressing her cheek. "You are a tenderhearted woman. Your dad sees that in you."

Erika caught her breath, already missing his touch when he moved his hand.

"I hope I didn't overstep with what I said."

Her heart pattered in her chest. "No."

Peyton lowered his voice. "Have you approached your father about how you feel?"

She nodded. "Yes, a couple of times and he always changes the subject. He's not willing to discuss the situation. How are we supposed to solve our problems if he won't talk about them?" She bit her lip.

Peyton ran his fingers over her hand, making her heart pound. "Give it time. I'd say the issue lies with him. Maybe one of these days your father will open up."

His words chimed in her heart like miniature bells jingling in the breeze. Was there really hope she and her father would come to an understanding?

Again, Peyton stiffened his muscles, shooing away the strong urge to hold her, to kiss away her concerns. He had to admit, he didn't understand her father's attitude. But he intended to pray about it.

The rumble of Mr. Ford's ATV notified him that someone was approaching from the pastures.

Chet stopped the vehicle on the road near them. "Hey, Peyton, Erika."

"How ya doing? You out touring the pastures?" Peyton asked.

"Naw. Mr. Ford sent me out to fill the feeder in the back pasture. Them sheep out there jest got their dinner. Fred's out roaming the pasture, ready to watch over the flock."

"Fred, the donkey." Peyton smiled. "Amazing how he can guard those creatures."

Erika tucked a strand of hair behind her ear. "Dad mentioned something about having Pete visit. You brothers have been apart too long."

Chet's eyes opened as round as one of Charlotte's pancakes. "I don't plan to waste a minute of my time with my brother. If I didn't know better, I'd think Someone is watching out for us."

"You got that right." Peyton looked from Chet to Erika as the words gushed out. "One of these days I'd like to run a ranch myself—a place for guys like you and Pete to live—as a family."

Erika gripped his arm. "Peyton, that would be wonderful."

Chet's grin spread across his face. "You can say that again."

Peyton peered at Chet a few seconds longer. Hope radiated from the kid's eyes. Peyton had gotten the boy's expectations up. Had he made the announcement too soon? Would he actually be able to accomplish his goal?

Chapter Eighteen

Friday morning, Erika grabbed her empty breakfast plate and set it in the kitchen sink. Dad had mentioned he wanted her to ride out to the north pasture to identify some quality grazing locations. Then he wanted her to estimate the number of sheep they could feasibly herd there. For once, Dad gave her a job demanding knowledge of the industry and sheep ranching. She rounded the corner out of the kitchen into the hall.

"Erika, could you do me a favor?" Dad met her in the hall. "I talked to the director at the boys' home and received permission to have Pete out this weekend. Could you please go into town and pick him up?"

Anticipation built in her chest. She was likely as excited as Chet would soon be. "Sure. I'll check the north pasture later this afternoon."

"That's fine. I only talked to the director a few minutes ago. And ask Peyton to go with you. Pete seemed to warm up to him when the boy was here for the fundraiser. I'd like to keep Pete's arrival a surprise for Chet." He headed toward his office.

Peyton had encouraged her to open up to Dad. Now was as good a time as any. "Got a second?"

Dad peered at her as if trying to figure out what she would say. "Sure, let's talk in my office."

Closing the doors, her father sank into the chair behind his desk. "Sit over there, sweetie." He pointed to the chair adjacent to the desk. "What's going on?"

Erika perched on the corner of the office chair and took a deep breath. Hopefully, she could frame the words in a way he'd understand her thoughts.

Dad folded his hands in front of him. "From the look on your face, I'd say this is serious."

She wrapped a strand of hair around her finger. "I'll come out with it. When I went to visit Grandma and Grandpa the other day, Grandpa talked about Aunt Rebekah. The conversation began a chain of thoughts in my mind."

"Oh? Grandpa can be a talker sometime." Her father glanced at something over her head.

Just like Dad to divert the conversation from what she needed to discuss. "We never seem to talk about her. Every time I bring up her name, I feel as if you change the subject." This conversation took courage, but this time she told him her thoughts.

Dad shifted in his seat. "Look. My sister's memory lies here." He tapped his chest over his heart. "But what good does it do to talk about her?"

Erika firmed her lips. "You had the privilege of knowing her. I didn't. Can't you share some of your boyhood with me? What was she like? What are your favorite memories of her?" She drummed her fingers on the chair's arm.

Her father frowned and fiddled with a paper clip on top of his desk.

"Dad?" She shook her head. "Do you talk about her

to Mom or the boys?" What was it about Aunt Rebekah he didn't want to discuss?

She bit her lip until it hurt. "I better go to town to pick up Pete." She walked out the outer door to look for Peyton.

"Erika," Dad called.

She turned toward his office. "Yeah?"

"I love you very much, but can we let this subject go?" He spoke quietly as if uttering the words pained him.

Erika shook her head. Other families experienced tragedies in their lives. They relied on each other for healing and support. Why would Dad close off that part of his life from her?

Peyton pointed to his car. "You want to take mine for a change?"

Erika nodded. "That's fine. Thanks for going with me."

"I need to fire up the old buggy every so often anyway." They walked behind the bunkhouse where his Chevy was parked. He scurried around to the passenger side to open the door for Erika. Might as well show her ranch hands could be gentlemen.

As they sailed down the highway to Oakville, Peyton caught a glance of Erika and looked back to the road again. She gripped her fists into tight balls and wore a frown.

"Okay, what's going on?" He'd only recently spoken to her about her issue with her father. Did it related to the advice he'd given her to open up to him?

She shrugged. "I tried to speak to Dad. He said he couldn't talk about that part of his life."

"I'm not a psychologist, but if I were to guess, there's more to what your father is saying—or not saying." He patted her hand resting on the seat. "Be patient. He'll eventually talk about your aunt Rebekah."

"Maybe." She wrapped her arms around her chest and scooted down in the passenger seat.

"I'm sorry. I know your dad's attitude hurts, but I can guarantee, the problem isn't yours."

"Do you really believe that?"

"Yes, emphatically." He reached to grip her hand.

Erika lowered her voice, her tone quiet yet determined. "Someday, when I have kids, I hope I can communicate with them better than Dad and I do."

He cleared his throat. Erika had no way of knowing the pain her statement had caused in his gut. Someday, if he had a second chance to be a father, he'd feel the same.

Chapter Nineteen

Sunday afternoon, Peyton gazed again at his mother's face on the video call. "Love you, Mom."

"Love you, too, son. Thank you for calling."

Peyton hung up the phone and walked out of the bunkhouse and into the bright sun. Only until he talked to her did he realized how much he missed her. *Thank You, Lord, for giving me such a beautiful mother.*

He leaned on the trunk of the giant oak in front of the bunkhouse, watching Chet demonstrate to Pete how to lasso a calf. Except this was no cow but a tree stump.

"See, Pete. It's easy." Chet whirled the rope above his head and tossed.

Chet's tow-headed brother doubled over with laughter. "You missed that cow. Better try again."

Peyton gazed toward the sky and remembered what Mr. Ford said Friday after Pete arrived at the ranch. "You boys want free time around the ranch instead of mucking the stables, then you've got to go to church with the family." Hope spread through Peyton's chest. The two brothers attended and even seemed to listen to the pastor.

Peyton rubbed his stomach, full after the delicious meal of fried chicken, mashed potatoes and gravy, corn on the cob, and lemon pie—like Mama used to make after church.

"Yahoo." Chet hollered as he pulled the loop tightly over the stump. "See. I done it."

Peyton shook his head and then grinned. If only he could get ahold of that boy and teach him better grammar.

"Come on, Chet. Let's go see them sheep." Pete took off toward the sheep barn in a sprint.

Chet looped the rope around and tied it off. "Yeah, sure. In a minute."

Mr. Ford drove up in the ATV and stopped in front of Chet. "Remember when I sent you out to fill the feeders the other day?"

A frown furrowed Chet's brow. "Yeah?"

"Did you forget something?" Mr. Ford's expression said that his next words weren't going to be complimentary.

"Er, I don't think so."

"I just rode out there, and the gate to the north pasture was wide open. Sheep could come or go at will. Do you think that's a good idea?"

Peyton had become used to the rancher's rough reprimands, but Chet hadn't been here long enough to know he treated all the hands the same.

Chet dropped his chin to his chest. "N… no. I thought I closed it."

"Well, you didn't. Your memory needs to improve—one hundred percent." The ATV rumbled as Mr. Ford sped away.

Peyton supposed that it was possible someone else had gone out later and had forgotten to close the gate. Possible, but not likely. He hadn't and to his knowledge, Mac hadn't ridden out anytime in the last couple of days. Certainly, Austin and Jace wouldn't make that kind of mistake.

Chet gripped his fingers into balls. His face scarlet, he pinched his lips and turned to march into the bunkhouse.

Peyton followed him in. The young man needed a talking to. "Chet, got a moment?"

Chet reached under his bed and threw his backpack onto the bedspread. He pulled out a few shirts, some shoes, and a toiletry kit from a drawer in his cabinet. "That's all I get from that man. One scolding after another. I'm not stayin' where I'm not wanted."

Peyton sat on Chet's bed next to his backpack. "Take a breath. Count to ten. And then we'll talk."

Chet peered at Peyton. "You think you know it all?" He plopped a ball cap on his head and picked up a little book ready to toss it in with his other things.

"What's that, buddy?" Peyton pointed to the book. He caught a glimpse of the first two words of the title— The Little.

"Nothin'." Chet grabbed his backpack and scooted it farther away from Peyton.

Peyton gripped Chet's arm. "Whoa. Stop a minute."

Chet breathed in and then out. "One, two, three … "

"All right." Peyton nodded. "Now sit down here, and let's talk." He patted the bed beside him.

Chet slipped down, his lower lip hanging out a mile.

"May I give you some advice?"

"You're going to anyway." He shrugged but lifted his gaze to Peyton.

"Sometimes Mr. Ford uses a rough tone of voice which can get a guy's attention. He's done it to me quite a few times. You've about reached manhood, if I were to guess, so I consider you a man. Old enough to act like one, too."

A grin spread on Chet's lips, and he nodded. "Tomorrow's my birthday. I'll be eighteen. Officially on my own."

Peyton shook his hand. "Happy birthday. That's all the more reason it's time for you to prove to others you're an adult. Mr. Ford has every right to ask you to remember to close the gate, so take his instructions like a grownup."

Chet tucked his ballcap down farther on his forehead. "I guess you're right."

"I remember a few weeks ago when you forgot to secure the equipment in the back of the truck. I took the fall for you, but it's time for you to grow up and become responsible for yourself. You've got a brother now who needs someone to look up to."

Chet nodded. "I know you're trying to steer me in the right direction. Only thing is, I'm scared to tell Mr. Ford it's my eighteenth birthday. I lied to him when I first came to the ranch. I told him I was already eighteen."

Peyton slapped the kid on the shoulder. "See, you've got two opportunities to prove your manhood. Take your boss's reprimand like an adult and then go to him and confess your lie."

Chet frowned. "But what if he fires me?"

"If he does, he does. Something tells me he won't if you ask for forgiveness." Peyton shooed Chet with the back of his hands. "Go. You can do this."

"Will you go with me?"

As they entered the ranch's office, Peyton gave Chet a thumbs up. "You can do this," he mouthed.

"Can I talk to you a minute?" A flush crept across Chet's cheeks as he stood before Mr. Ford at his desk.

The boss looked up from his computer. "Yes, go ahead."

Chet opened his mouth and closed it again. He shuffled from one foot to the other as he stared at the floor.

Peyton poked Chet in his ribs.

Chet looked up and cleared his throat. "You see, sir. I need to say I'm sorry about leaving the gate open. I'll try not to let it happen again." His Adam's apple bobbed up and down.

The boss covered his mouth with one hand, likely trying to disguise a grin. "Thank you, Chet. I appreciate that."

The freckles dotting Chet's cheeks looked darker on his red face. "One more thing, sir. I need to make a confession. When you hired me, I lied about my age. I'll be eighteen tomorrow. I'm really sorry now that I didn't tell the truth."

Without a change in expression, the older man nodded. "I figured as much, son."

"Then … then I'm not fired?" Chet gulped.

Mr. Ford folded his arms over his chest. "No, as long as you promise to start acting like a man and showing some accountability."

Chet smiled, some of the red on his cheeks fading. "Yes, sir. I'll try my best. You see, I'm grateful to you for giving me a chance." He turned to glance at Peyton. "My buddy, here, is helping me understand what it means to grow up."

Mr. Ford shook Chet's hand and grinned. "Very good. He's an excellent example to follow."

Peyton's heart warmed at Mr. Ford's reassurance. He supposed Chet needed that same kind of encouragement. "All right." Peyton clapped Chet's shoulder. "Let's go back to the bunkhouse and clean up the mess you made."

In the hands' quarters, Chet unpacked his backpack. He folded the shirts and neatly placed them in his chest of drawers. Then he pulled out the book with the title Peyton had partially viewed.

"May I ask what you're reading?"

He shoved his hands into his pockets. "Oh, I'm not reading this. It's something my mom gave me a long time ago. I keep it with me all the time. I can remember her like that … instead of the way she was later."

Peyton blinked. "May I see it?" He couldn't imagine what would be so special to the kid, now becoming an adult.

Chet held out the book to him as if he shared a prized possession. "*The Little Engine That Could*. She used to read it to me when I was younger."

Warmth spread through Peyton's heart with the memory. As a child, he'd requested the story when his mom read to him before bed. "I know that book. I used to read it also. Great message. Never give up. I believe that's what you did today."

Chet thrust out his chest and smiled. "I guess I did."

Pete strolled into the bunkhouse. "Hey, Chet. When are you coming to the barn?"

Peyton turned to walk out the door. "See you later, guys." Now to talk to Erika about the idea that had popped into his head.

Erika placed her index finger on her lips. "Okay, everyone. Quiet. He's coming around the house." The afternoon breeze lifted a strand of her hair off her cheek.

Peyton escorted a blindfolded Chet alongside Pete to the backyard and pulled the scarf off his eyes.

"Surprise." The family and ranch hands roared in unison. "Happy birthday."

The boy's mouth fell open as he peered around at the sight in front of him.

A table covered with a bright blue tablecloth and brimming with a chocolate cake, vanilla ice cream, lemonade, and Mom's homemade cookies no doubt caught his eye.

"I—I—thank you, everybody." He swallowed a lump in his throat and sniffed, probably fighting tears.

After Peyton's quick explanation about Chet's birthday, a small party was the least they could do. Her heart sang. She and Peyton had worked together to honor a boy who likely hadn't celebrated his birthday since becoming a teen. A sense of joy filled her as she witnessed the light in his eyes.

For two hours, Chet seemed to relish the picture taking, blowing out the candles on his cake, and merely being the center of attention. The wide grin on his face when he bit into a large piece of chocolate cake with creamy chocolate icing said it all.

After the celebration, Dad caught up with her as she helped clear the picnic table. He touched her shoulder. "Sweetie, there's something I need to talk to you about. I'm sorry I waited this long, but ranch business has bogged me down."

Did he finally want to explain more about the aunt she never knew? And why would he choose now to talk to her? "Sure."

He led her to the outdoor chairs at the edge of the lawn and extended his hand for her to take a seat.

Dad slipped down beside her. "Peyton suggested several steps we could take here at the ranch to increase our revenue."

Her hopes fell into her stomach, and she sighed. Not at all the topic she expected.

"One is attending a trade show to speak face-to-face with potential customers." He patted her arm. "Your mom and I have plans to go to Las Vegas in a couple of weeks. I'd like for you to run the ranch while I'm gone."

Erika's heart picked up speed. "Me, all alone?" But wasn't this what she'd wanted? A chance to prove to her father she could manage the ranch without his supervision for a while? "I mean, sure, I can do it."

Her father rubbed the back of his neck. "The only thing is Jace and Charlotte are taking a little time off to visit her mother in San Antonio. Austin is going with us, so that leaves the other ranch hands. Sure you can handle things?"

Erika swallowed hard. She finally had a chance to show her father she could manage the ranch. And she'd better not make a careless mistake.

Chapter Twenty

Two weeks into May and Mom and Dad had left three days ago. Erika stroked Paint's neck and glanced at the sky beyond the pasture. The dark cloud tops and flickering lightening concerned her. Earlier a breeze had sent soft puffs of air around the pasture. Now the wind kicked up and swirled, tossing hair into her face.

She lifted the strands, tucked them behind her ear, and pulled her hat down tighter. While she always relished the rain, she figured this storm with its intensity of lightning and wind, could be a cause for concern. She hoped that the bulk of the approaching weather event would veer off in another direction.

A bee brushed Erika's face, and she flicked it away. Patting Paint's mane, she smiled. The storm would pass in the same way her dad's financial stress was resolving, thanks to Peyton.

Running a ranch—easy.

She tightened her shoulders. Who was she kidding? She couldn't do it alone without the ranch hands. Getting ahead of the rain, she inspected the last of the fence line for today and spurred her horse to return to the ranch office to wait out the storm and to help

Peyton finish up the paperwork for the new order.

She led Paint into his stall at the horse barn and filled his trough with hay and his bucket with water. Strolling toward the house, she sniffed the air. The aroma of impending rain filtered through her nose—a scent she didn't ordinarily smell. At the side entrance to the office, she peered into the window.

Chewing the end of a pencil, Peyton pored over papers on her father's desk and then switched his gaze to the computer. His loyalty to her father and the ranch impressed her—a trait not everyone possessed.

How many times had he endeared himself to her? But on each occasion, in some small manner, he'd mentioned his faith. She believed in the Lord, but not in the same passionate way as Peyton. The desire to know more tugged at her heart.

Peyton looked up when she walked in. "Hey. I answered an email. We have an additional client who'd like to do business. A small yarn producing company in east Texas."

Peyton's full lips and powerful shoulders set Erika's heart pounding. She couldn't ignore or deny her attraction to him much longer. She moved behind him to glance over his shoulder at the email. His nearness sparked a magnetic pull. She took a long, delicious breath of the earthy aroma of sandalwood.

An offensive, blaring sound carried across the room, and she flinched. She glanced up at Dad's display cabinet. On top, red lights flashed.

Peyton jumped up from the office chair, sending it spinning. "A NOAA radio alert."

Erika held her breath. "Could it be a tornado? This is the season, unfortunately."

She froze as the announcement came. "This is a NOAA radio alert. The national weather service in Dallas, Texas has issued a warning for central Texas to include the following counties: Murphy, Everly, and Oakville. Expect winds up to one hundred and fifty miles an hour, damage to roofs and uprooted trees. Take cover now."

Peyton rushed toward her. "Erika, that's us. Oakville County."

"We've got to get the sheep into the barn—now."

The wind flung sand into Erika's eyes, and she blinked. Above, a dark cloud crept toward the ranch from the southwest. Erika grasped her throat. "Mac left for town a couple of hours ago. He said he needed to buy groceries."

Peyton frowned. "He'll take cover in Oakville."

"Yes, but that leaves you, me, and Chet at the ranch." Erika bounded out the office door. "We've got to shelter the sheep. We can't take any chances."

Peyton tugged his hat off, ran a hand through his hair, and set his Stetson on his head again. "We can do this together."

Chet rounded the sheep barn in a sprint. "A tornado warning." He gripped his phone in one hand. "I'll get the ranch equipment into the storage building."

"Thanks, Chet." The wind picked up, and Erika shivered. Another weather warning when she was a teen darted into her memory. An F1 tornado that hadn't touched down at the ranch. But would her father's property fare as well this time?

The eerie black cloud continued to advance, shrouding the sky with darkness. Toward the north pasture, howling gusts bent the trees to a forty-five-degree angle.

Peyton raced by her side as they bolted into the sheep pen.

Erika hollered for her border collie. "Come, Sam."

The dog charged up behind the fold to coax them in the opposite direction—to the opening in the barn.

Peyton and Sam rounded up the few stragglers on the other side of the pen.

After the last animal had trotted into the barn, Erika glanced at the sky. The ominous black cloud crawled closer toward the ranch. She wiped her brow. "The horses are in the horse barn so I think we're ready. We have a tornado shelter in the basement of the house. Let's take cover there."

Chet returned from the storehouse and ran toward them.

Peyton nodded. "Sam, Chet, let's go." He beckoned them to follow.

Erika raced behind and then froze. "Peyton," she screamed. " Jace and Austin left some of the flock. In the north pasture."

Peyton gulped. "Chet, go on into the shelter. We'll be back shortly."

"Save us a seat." Erika's meager attempt at humor didn't produce smiles. "Let's take the ATV."

Peyton sprinted to the equipment shed and returned with the vehicle. "Do you think we'll have time to outrun this storm?"

Panic surged and grabbed her stomach. "I can't

leave those sheep in the pasture. It's almost a third of the flock." She shouted over the sound of rushing wind. "If something happened to them, the ranch could be in danger of closing down. We've got to get the sheep back to the barn."

Peyton gripped the ATV's steering wheel, the vehicle dipping and rolling along the dirt road toward the north pasture. He gulped down the anxiety in his chest. Though Dallas had a few tornadoes in his time, he'd never been caught in the middle of one.

Black clouds continued to advance from the southwest, almost overhead now. The wind tossed the ATV from side to side.

Toward the right, a large flock of sheep huddled near the fence.

Using the same approach as before, they coaxed Sam to maneuvered the flock toward the ranch as he and Erika rode along in the ATV.

"Over there." Erika pointed to the right.

Three ewes stood frozen in place.

Erika yelled. "Sam, find!"

The border collie ran toward the small group. As if awaking from a trance, they loped toward the rest of the sheep.

Peyton lifted the hood of his jacket over his head as huge drops of rain splattered his face and shoulders.

Erika grasped his arm. "Peyton, we have to hurry."

By instinct, the sheep picked up speed and trotted down the road to the barn.

Pulling up at the sheep barn, Peyton jumped out.

Erika bolted from the ATV and opened the door.

The creatures crowded in, bleating and baaing, as if home never looked so good.

Peyton's stomach jolted. "Erika, where's Sam?" He glanced toward the sky and then sucked in a breath. From the black mass now overhead, a rotating column of air extended from the cloud downward heading in the direction of the north pasture moving toward them.

Erika's eyes widened, and she shook her head. "We have to take shelter now."

The loud whirring, like a train zooming by, confirmed her words.

Fear and regret shone in Erika's eyes. "We have a root cellar in the barn. That will be the safest place for us." She glanced around at the main section of the enclosure. "I don't see Sam."

Peyton wrapped his arm around her shoulders. "He'll be fine. Let's go." He could only wish he spoke the truth. Erika loved the dog. But what would happen if he didn't make it to shelter?

Erika led them to the center of the barn, the whirling louder. She lifted a handle on the floor and raised the door to the cellar.

A ladder led to the bottom.

"Arf." Sam raced toward them.

"Awe, Sam." Erika's voice broke.

"He's here." Peyton grabbed the collie in his arms, breathed in the musty cool air, and started down the ladder.

At the bottom, Sam scampered to the inside wall, as if he knew the best place to wait out the danger.

Erika jumped down the last two steps and headed

toward Sam.

Peyton snickered. "I'm glad your dog decided to join us."

Erika grasped an old quilt, tossed it on the floor, and hunkered down.

Peyton knelt and slipped his arm around her, trying to ignore the ominous rumbling above.

Sam rose from his spot, padded closer, and burrowed between them.

Erika stroked Sam's fur. "The Ford ranch has to survive. The future of my family depends on it."

Peyton rubbed Sam's head. "The animals are safe. Whatever happens, God will see us through."

When she gripped his hand tighter, a sense overcame him. He wanted to protect her, to be by her side. But was Peyton ready to put the past behind him and begin a new life?

Chapter Twenty-One

The morning sun shone through the narrow window as Peyton returned to the root cellar and inhaled a slow breath of moist, cool air. The faint aroma of onions and garlic caused his stomach to growl. He turned his gaze toward Erika. Her closed eyes and soft rise and fall of her chest told him she slept.

Sam stirred and licked Erika's cheek.

She rubbed her eyes, sat up straight, and patted Sam's head. A disheveled strand of hair fell into her face, and she brushed it from her pale skin. "I think the storm's past. We better check on Chet and the ranch."

"Don't worry. We're safe." He gave her a hand up. "I didn't want to wake you so I checked on Chet a while ago. He's in the bunkhouse now."

She rushed toward the ladder. "What about the house and the barns?" She climbed the rungs leading to the first floor.

Peyton followed, lifting Sam up the ladder.

Erika hurried out the barn door into the quiet morning, the air now an eerie calm. She looked toward the bunkhouse, then the family home, and then the tool shed and horse barn. "I don't think the high winds made impact with any of the buildings." She took a few steps toward the equipment storage and the tool shed. "Only a couple of downed trees toward the east, on the other side of Jace's house."

Peyton caught up with her and stood by her side.

She leaned next to him, her shoulder against his chest as she exhaled a long breath. "It's okay now. We're fine."

"Good thing you remembered the sheep in the north pasture." He slipped his arms around her shoulders again. "You did a good job of seeing the ranch through a violent tornado."

"I didn't do it alone." She turned in his arms to face him. "Chet and Sam were there." She whispered. "And you." She rested against him.

Then her eyes widened. She twisted away and raced to the sheep barn again. "What about the ewes and lambs? Are they okay? We need to go back and check."

Peyton caught up with her and grasped her hand. "Erika, everything's okay. When I went to find Chet, the animals were fine. They may be a little rattled, but they survived. I think they felt secure in their pens." But would she believe him?

She swept her hand over her forehead. "I need to see for myself."

Peyton shrugged and followed the persistent woman into the barn. Did she have a stubborn side he hadn't observed before?

She ran up and down the stalls and then slowed when she arrived at Sadie's pen where Sadie's lamb peacefully nursed.

Erika stared at the ewe and her offspring, her hand on her throat. As if struggling to breathe, her chest rose and fell.

Something was going on, but what? Peyton had given up trying to fully understand women—especially this one. He stood next to her, hoping in moments she'd explain what bothered her.

She mumbled in a hushed tone. "Peyton …"

"Everything's okay."

"No." She ran her hands through her hair.

Peyton blinked. What had she realized that he had not. "What? What are you trying to say?"

Her tears fell.

Peyton peered at her, wishing he could read her mind. What was wrong? He stepped closer in order to hear her muffled words.

"If I had died in the storm, I'm not sure what would've happened."

"If you'd died? You mean where you'd spend eternity?" Peyton waited, not sure of how she'd answer. He took a deep breath.

She cupped her hands on her cheeks. "You're so passionate about your faith in God. So sure of Him. As we brought the last of the flock into the barn and hurried to the root cellar, I thought—what if I die in this storm. I don't know what comes next."

"What do you mean?"

"What would've happened if I'd been killed by a falling tree or crushed under the debris of the barn." More tears fell. "I don't know God the way you do. I wouldn't spend the next life with Him."

Peyton's heart thundered. This woman was asking him how to find a relationship with God. His spirit soared as he gripped her hand. "It's so easy. Just tell God you're sorry for the things you've done wrong in the past and tell Him you believed Jesus took the punishment you deserved."

Erika lifted her wet lashes to him and murmured. "Help me tell Him."

Peyton coaxed Erika to kneel beside him at Sadie's pen. With a soft voice, she repeated every word after him.

Afterward, they arose, and she laid her head on his shoulder. "I'll never forget this day. Thank you for showing me how to have a relationship with God.

As if Erika carried a heavy bag of animal feed on her shoulders and then offloaded the weight onto the table in the horses' barn, her arms felt light. She opened her mouth to tell the sheep what had just happened—about the change in her life, but then she closed her lips and only grinned.

Peyton squeezed her hand. "God loves you so much. He wants you to learn more about Him. Life will still have problems, but the Lord will walk through each day with you."

Erika covered her mouth and giggled. "It took a tornado to help me understand."

"God is creative in that way." Peyton tightened the lock on Sadie's pen and grinned. "He touches our lives in lots of ways. I had a friend who saw a Christian movie that made her think. Later, another friend called, and my friend prayed right there on the phone to ask Jesus into her life."

"That's exciting. I'm happy for your friend." Erika paused, gaining time to collect her thoughts. "We're fortunate. The ranch house and buildings are intact."

Peyton turned from the pen to face her. "No one could've done a better job."

"Thanks to the Lord."

Erika ran toward Chet when she spotted him exiting the bunkhouse. "You're safe." She hugged him.

"In your basement at the main house, I got scared at first. Then I thought about you and Peyton. I didn't know if you'd made it back from the pasture or not." He hugged her back. "I asked God to protect all of us."

"Thank you, Chet. I believe He did." Their beautiful, intact home stood as a testimony to divine intervention. And her new faith in God.

"Guess it takes a tornado to help us realize what things in life are most important." Chet eyes sparkled with his realization.

Erika patted his back. "I'd say you're getting to be pretty wise."

"Yeah? Well, maybe I am." The teen poked out his chest.

Erika giggled at the boy's newfound confidence.

Peyton, Sam following, walked up from the barn.

Erika turned to Peyton with a smile. She'd never known a guy like him, at least not in Oakville—someone who'd remain by her side when things got tough. "We need to check the west and north pastures—to assess the possible damage."

"I'll be right back with the ATV." Chet raced toward the equipment shed. "Come on, Sam."

Sam barked his happy yap and raced beside him.

Five minutes later, Chet returned with the vehicle, Sam perched next to him in the passenger seat.

Peyton scooted into the back, and Erika sat in the front, her arm around Sam.

She held onto the collie a little tighter than she should've, tension beginning to build in her stomach. They'd seen the funnel touch ground. Though their house and barns were safe, maybe the pastures weren't.

The section of the north pasture nearest the ranch house looked intact. They drove farther down the dirt road, and then Erika caught her breath as she looked toward the left.

As if a giant lawnmower had cut a straight line through the pasture, the lovely old oak trees lay on their sides, roots exposed. A path of bushes and grass were uprooted and resting at odd angles.

Chet pointed to his right. "Look at them trees over there."

The grove of ash, redbuds, and pecan trees lay horizontal and on the ground.

Erika clasped her chest. "The path of the tornado. Looks like it came from the north and then veered to the east before reaching the ranch."

Peyton smiled. "I think we can thank God for that."

"You're right." Erika believed him. His words were not mere platitudes but true. God had saved their ranch.

Chet's stomach growled. "I hate to say it, but tornados make me hungry. What's to eat?"

Erika patted Sam's head. "Maybe Mac left something in the fridge before he went shopping in Oakville."

Peyton spoke from behind her. "I'm sure he's fine.

He should be back soon."

"In the meantime, we're all hungry." Erika laughed. "What do you say if I cook up something to eat?"

"You know how to cook, Miss Erika?" Chet turned the ATV around and headed back to the ranch.

Erika laughed. "Of course, I do. Right Sam?"

Chet let out a howl. "Feeding Sam ain't the same as feeding us men."

Peyton rubbed his belly. "True. I'll help you, Erika."

"Now we're really in trouble." Chet steered the ATV around a pothole. "Peyton don't know how to cook."

"He probably knows his way around the kitchen better than me." Erika smiled. "I confess I'm not an expert."

In front of the main house, Erika stepped out and glanced at Peyton. "I suppose I better call Dad and let him know everything is okay."

As if the phone had heard, her cell jingled with Dad's ring. "Hi, Dad. How's Las Vegas?" For sure, he'd heard about the weather by now.

"Are you all right?" With a tone louder than usual, the words blared in her ear. "I saw the news on TV."

Warmth radiated through Erika's chest. Dad had asked about her first, instead of the ranch. "I'm fine, Dad. Peyton, Chet and I took shelter in the basement of the house and the cellar."

"What about the ranch?" His tone tightened with each word.

"The tornado made a turn to the east before it made contact with the buildings. Peyton says we were blessed by God's protection."

Silence met her ears for a moment. "Dad?"

"I'm so glad."

She needed to offer more assurance. "Peyton and I were able to get the sheep from the north pasture and into the barn moments before the tornado touched down."

Silence met her ear again, and then Dad's voice carried over the phone. "Wonderful. That's real good news, Erika girl. Good thing Peyton was there to take care of you and oversee the crisis."

Erika's heart sped up. Dad acknowledged Peyton's protection, which he well deserved. If she had her way, he would've included her in those accolades. But the important thing was that the Ford ranch was safe from harm.

Chapter Twenty-two

In the horse barn the next day, Erika gripped the shovel filled with soiled shavings and tossed the contents into the wheelbarrow. She dumped the dirty water from the buckets behind the barn and filled each with fresh, clean water from the garden hose.

The sound of Sam's happy bark and an engine caught her attention. She peeked out the stall's window, and her heart pounded. Dad and Mom stepped out of the truck they'd taken to the airport.

She tossed her gloves on the worktable and tucked her shirt into her jeans. Had they found any potential customers in Las Vegas? She wanted to believe they had.

The bowl filled with large chunks of beef, slices of carrots, onions, and peppers, and a thick sauce tempted Peyton's appetite. He hadn't realized how hungry he was until he sat down at the meal. He glanced at Chet and Mac across from him at the hands' table in the dining room. "Mac, you outdid yourself."

"I second that." At the family table, Erika took another piece of cornbread from the platter and lathered it with butter.

"Mac, you were a lifesaver, stepping in and cooking today." Mrs. Ford glanced toward their table. "I'm still unpacking from our trip."

"Glad to do it, ma'am." Mac took a sip of his iced tea.

Chet laughed. "Like I said before, tornadoes can make a man hungry."

"You ever decide to give up ranching, you can always work as a chef." Peyton said.

Mac shook his head and rubbed his hands on his rough cotton apron which he'd tied around his waist. "Not sure if you'd like my liver and onions that I serve with collard greens."

Peyton reached for the plate of apple pie. "In any case, I'm mighty grateful you rode out the storm safely in Oakville."

"Yeah. Only stayed in the shelter for a couple of hours. I was on my way back to the ranch before I knew it." Mac glanced at Mr. Ford. "Need another serving, sir?"

"No thanks, Mac." Mr. Ford took the last bite of his slice of apple pie. "I talked to Mom and Dad earlier. The tornado didn't reach Oakville. She said they only saw high winds and some rain."

"You never know what the weather will do." Peyton wiped his mouth with the edge of his napkin. "How did the trip go? Any possible clients?"

"Overall, I'm pleased with the results of the Las Vegas trip. We made several lucrative contacts." Mr. Ford glanced at Peyton sitting at the hands' table. "Your ideas proved effective, Peyton."

Peyton swallowed the last of his piece of pie and nodded. "I figured attending the Nevada show would be worthwhile." Praise felt good, of course, and he wanted to see the ranch prosper. But what about Erika? Had her father given her the thanks due her?

Chapter Twenty-three

After lunch two days later, Erika pushed her chair away from the table and firmed her lips. It was finally time. "Dad, may I speak with you in your office?" Dad had rested up for several days now. Erika figured he'd had adequate time to recuperate from the trip.

Mr. Ford frowned but stood from the table. "Okay."

Erika approached the dining room door. Determination fortified her, and she pressed her lips into a straight line.

Then a knot rose in her stomach. Their last conversation about Aunt Rebekah hadn't gone well. Would today be any different?

Inside the office, Dad closed the door and studied her face. "I believe I know what you want to discuss."

The chicken stew she'd eaten began to protest in her stomach. After she confronted him, was Dad going to tell her once again that he couldn't discuss the subject now? She couldn't wait any longer to talk about what was on her mind. "I'll get straight to my point. I fully expect to take over this ranch someday and wanted to be as prepared as possible. I need your support." Merely saying the words felt good.

He stared at his boots for a moment and then met her gaze. "You're right."

Erika sat up straight. She hadn't expected him to say that.

"It's something we need to get out in the open, and I'm mostly to blame."

She gazed at her father, his words making little sense.

Dad folded his hands under his chin. "Forgive me, Erika, for the past, for always pushing you away from ranch responsibilities to kitchen duties or other tasks in the house." He shook his head, a slight smile filling his lips. "Not that kitchen duties aren't important. We couldn't do without your mother and Charlotte's cooking skills."

Erika couldn't muster the same smile her father wore. "True, and I admire Mom and Charlotte. But as I said, I need to be ready for the day when I run this ranch. I want to continue training to work outdoors, to ride the fence line or muck out the horses' stalls or sheer sheep."

Dad drew in a long breath. "For several years now, I've tried to ignore that fact."

"But why?" A slow ache began in her neck.

"There's so much we need to talk about." He pointed to the office chair. "Please sit down." He took the chair adjacent to her. "While we were in Las Vegas, I began to better understand your skills around the ranch."

Erika frowned. "What are you talking about?"

"Mac emailed me after the weather service spotted the tornado. He explained how he was trapped in town in the storm shelter and couldn't risk returning to the ranch."

"Oh?" What did that have to do with anything? Erika rubbed the back of her neck.

"He said he tried texting you to see how things were going, but the winds must've affected your cell service. He texted Peyton next, and fortunately, his phone was still working. Peyton described how you'd instigated the last-minute trip to the north pasture to round up the sheep Jace and Austin had taken out a few days before. And the whole time you kept your wits about you. He said your confidence and calm encouraged him." Dad stared at his feet again. "I'm sorry. It took someone else's reminder to bring me to my senses." He grasped both her hands.

For a moment, Erika figured she'd fallen asleep and dreamed Dad spoke the words. But, no, he sat squarely in front of her. His large, strong hands gripped hers.

"When we were in Las Vegas, I realized there was nothing I could do to help you. I felt paralyzed, unable to take care of the property that our family had owned for generations. I knew I had to trust you to do the job. At the same time, I came to the realization that you're a strong woman. I thought back about the many times you rounded up the sheep, repaired fences, and took care of the horses."

Words she'd wanted to hear for years. Erika rested her hands in her lap. But what had made the difference?

Dad's shoulders slumped. "But there's something I should've settled a long time ago."

Erika's palms became moist. "What is it?"

He swallowed hard. "I knew this day would come. That I could no longer hide behind obscurity."

She raised her voice. "Dad, you're not explaining

yourself."

"I know, I know." Dad brushed a hand through his hair and cleared his throat. "I was trying to limit your work to responsibilities around the house."

She sat in silence. Had he taken back all the positive things he'd said?

He tapped his forehead. "I'm sorry. This is coming out all wrong."

Erika blinked. Though she loved her parent and wanted to remain respectful, controlling her words was getting harder by the minute.

He touched her hand. "Sweetie, I've always known how capable you are. You're a brave young woman. But you're still a woman."

Erika frowned. "What? You're holding my gender against me?"

"No, of course not. The issue relates to your Aunt Rebekah."

Erika sat on her hands, trying to remain calm. She had no idea where Dad was going with this.

"She fell from her horse that horrible day when she died, but you don't know the rest." His voice was brittle, like he strained to utter the words.

Erika stared at her father waiting for him to continue.

"You see, that day she was to take Coach out, the gentle horse she'd ridden since she was four. But his shoes were worn and in need of replacement. She was afraid if she rode him, he might get injured or lame."

Erika folded her hands. "Okay?"

"The day before, I was supposed to shoe Coach, and I forgot. Since I was fourteen, Mom and Dad trusted me to do the job." Dad gazed somewhere over Erika's head.

Dad's silence meant he decided not to go on. Then he spoke. "Rebekah took Lightening instead. She left the horse barn without telling your grandfather. Lightning was too much for her to handle. He bucked her off, and she hit her head on a rock. After she died," he swallowed hard, "I blamed myself. I've always blamed myself." He gripped the sides of his chair. "Mom and Dad trusted me. I let them down—and my sister. If only I had taken care of my responsibilities that day."

Erika's mouth dropped open, and she clutched his hand. "Dad, you can't fault yourself for that day. It was a horrible accident."

"I've always suffered this exhausting guilt. If only I had done my job, your aunt would still be alive." He shook his head back and forth. "I'm still ashamed of the mistake I made all those years ago."

Erika patted his shoulder. "I love you, Dad."

He swiped at the moisture on his face. "I believed if I could keep you at home and away from ranch animals and chores, I could keep you safe from the kind of harm that killed your Aunt Rebekah."

His thinking was illogical, a determination that began in his youth and carried on into adulthood. "We can't live our lives dominated by fear or regret."

Dad rubbed his forehead. "I know, but your mother and I had three sons who could take care of themselves, then you came along. You were my little girl, and I wanted to protect you. I realize now that my attempts to keep you safe were out of line—causing more trouble than I ever dreamed."

"But what about when we go to church? The pastor always talks about trusting God."

"Yes, but each time he spoke about faith in the Lord, I turned a deaf ear. I thought the advice didn't apply to me—that He couldn't forgive what I did. Recently, I realized how stupid my thinking has been. Can you forgive me?"

For the first time in her life, she understood. Her father only wanted to protect her because he loved her—and because of the loss of his sister. Warmth spread through her chest. "Yes, of course I do.'

Dad pulled her into his arms. "Oh, honey, I'm so glad we came to this understanding. I love you so much."

Erika remained in her father's embrace for a few more minutes and then sighed. Knowing the reason why he'd behaved as he did in the past was one thing. But would her father be able to put his words into action and encourage her to take care of the ranch chores alongside Jace and Austin?

Chapter Twenty-Four

The following Monday, Erika set out for the garden beyond the big house, bucket in tow. She slipped on her gardening gloves and glanced at the rows of green vegetables growing in the thriving garden. Charlotte would get all the credit for planting the fresh peas, spinach, cucumbers, and sweet potatoes they'd see in the fall—and she deserved the recognition.

Charlotte.

She'd seemed so different since the day Jace was bitten by the snake. Perhaps kinder, more relaxed.

Or maybe Erika had changed. Yesterday at church, the pastor's message on trust made sense. For once, she'd enjoyed singing along with the worship team instead of feeling awkward.

She bent down to pluck a couple of weeds that had invaded the area and tossed them into the bucket.

"Hey, Erika." Charlotte neared, her side-to-side gait indicating the additional weight she carried. "I'm so grateful you went to lunch with the rest of the family yesterday after church. I like this new Erika."

Erika had to admit she felt different. "I'm glad, too." Every time she looked at Charlotte, the old resentments didn't arise. Finding peace with Dad had made a difference, as well as her strengthened trust in God. She leaned down to pick a couple of weeds between the asparagus and the lettuce.

"You working in the garden?" She stared at Erika as if she didn't believe her eyes. "Thanks. That's a great help." She paused and patted her stomach. "I don't like to admit it, but lately it's harder for me to bend down to pull them."

Did Erika imagine Charlotte's face radiated red? "I'm glad I can help. Since the tornado, I'm more grateful than ever that our ranch is in intact, and we are all okay. How were things at your mom's house?"

"Good, except my mother nagged me the entire time about my weight. I pretended I didn't hear her." Charlotte wiped perspiration from her brow. "It's taken awhile, but I've finally admitted it's a problem."

Erika rose and set the bucket on the ground. "Is there something I can do to help?" Or maybe Charlotte would tell her to mind her own business.

Charlotte, face still red, grasped Erika's hand. "I'm sorry for the way I've treated you." Her chin trembled. "Honestly, I was jealous of you. You're so slender and cute. Everyone loves you. You're the apple of your papa's eye."

Erika paused a moment. How could they possibly hold such opposite opinions about the same subject? She gave an easy laugh. "I used to see things very differently. My relationship with Dad has only begun to resolve lately.

Chalotte placed her index finger on her cheek. "Can I trust you not to make fun of me? I need help. I want to become healthier—like you."

Erika's heart raced. She'd always thought Charlotte

considered herself better than her or a more important member of the family. "You know I will. Let's start by doing some exercises every day. Then we'll share our current eating habits and what we can do to make healthier choices." She grasped Charlotte's hand. "You're a beautiful woman. You can do this."

Charlotte slipped her arms around Erika and sniffed. "Thank you."

Later when Erika's bucket reached the rim with the unwanted weeds, she turned toward the burn pile where she'd dump them.

Still in awe of her conversation with her brother's wife, Erika pictured a slimmer version of her. But would Charlotte be able to change her lifestyle and get the healthy body she desired? She wouldn't get the shape she wanted unless she put her complete energy into the effort.

Peyton pitched a bale of hay into the hayfeeder behind the sheep barn and glanced up at the sound of footsteps.

"Been meaning to talk to you." Chet meandered toward Peyton, his hat perched on the back of his head. "Ever since that tornado, I been doing some thinkin."

"Sure." Peyton wiped off his hands and turned to face Chet. No doubt, he had something important to say, and Peyton had an inkling of what the subject matter might be.

"I was pert near scared out of my wits that day. You and Erika were in the barn, and I was all by myself.

Didn't even have Sam there."

Peyton nodded as he chewed on a blade of hay.

"For a long time, I didn't believe there was a God. Especially when my mother left me and Pete home alone all the time. I wondered how He could care about us, letting us go hungry like that."

"Chet—"

"Let me finish. He brought Mr. Ford into my life— and you. I see a change in Erika, too. Pete and I are together again, somethin' I never thought would happen."

"God's timetable is not always ours. I believe He allows us to go through things to grow us up, to mature us."

Chet scratched the back of his ear. "Suppose I could go to church with you and Erika next week?"

Peyton smiled. "You sure can." He hoped his interested in church would continue, or was this a passing phase?

Chapter Twenty-Five

First the shots and then a scream.

Peyton rushed toward her. He froze, paralyzed by the horror.

She lay on the muddy ground. So still.

He gathered her into his arms. "Please be okay." His voice broke with every syllable.

For a long moment, he swayed as he held her, praying he'd hear her say she was fine. He lowered his ear to her mouth.

Nothing.

He strained for a breath, as if he could breathe for her, yet air refused to enter his lungs. He gasped and sat up straight in bed. Perspiration rolled down his shoulders and arms. He escaped the confines of his blanket that held him captive and pushed through the door of the bunkhouse into the moist, summer night.

Outside, he heaved a breath of air. Panting, he willed his heart to slow.

Beyond the main house to the right, a faint light glowed.

Peyton tugged his t-shirt down over his warm-ups, slipped on his flip flops by the door, and took a few steps toward the light.

He stumbled forward as if tramping through a cloud of fog. Was he trekking through the depths of the jungle or on his way to the Ford's backyard? He wasn't sure.

He spotted a woman with long hair twirled into a knot on her head. She glided back and forth in the backyard swing, the light from a cell phone glowing. He no longer slept but gaped at Erika Ford on a ranch in central Texas.

Peyton took a few steps back. Now was not the time for a friendly conversation. He curved to return to the bunkhouse.

"Peyton, is that you?" Erika called, her soft tone reaching out to him in the dark night.

"Yeah. Out for a walk."

The high-pitched chirp of the katydids and crickets announced their presence in the starry night instead of the howls and yells of angry gold miners. No scuttle of badgers or hedgehogs or clicks of bats flitted overhead.

He meandered toward her. "You're up late."

"I couldn't sleep. You, too?"

He wished he hadn't slept. He wouldn't have traveled back to that time he'd struggled so hard to forget. "No, just a bad dream."

She scooted over on the swing and patted the seat. "Might as well sit. We can endure insomnia together."

Peyton could say no and return to his bunkhouse, but the risk of another nightmare was likely. It had happened before—two unpleasant dreams in one night launching him on an emotional roller coaster. He dropped down into the empty space and rested his hands on his knees.

"Care to talk about it? The dream, I mean."

Wasn't it about time he shared his struggle with her?

But was he ready to talk about how Sandra died? With a long draw of the evening air, he heard himself mutter. "Yes."

From the look on Peyton's face, Erika knew something had gone wrong. Was it a dream, as he said? "I've shared so much about myself. I consider you a good friend. I don't intend to repeat anything you say."

Peyton nodded. "Thank you."

He sat silent for another minute. Perhaps he'd changed his mind. Then quiet words emerged. "It was only last year."

Erika's heart beat faster. His elevated tone of voice offered the clue. This was painful for him.

"After college, I worked in a corporate job in Dallas. Two-piece suits, the works. I got married later, and after a few years, an opportunity arose at my church to serve full time in the jungles of Peru."

"You took the job in Peru?"

"Yes. I resigned from my position in Dallas. Sandra and I went through training and worked as missionaries in the Peruvian jungle."

"Sandra, your wife?"

He nodded. "Sandra was a trained nurse. We got word that many of the Peruvian gold miners were dying of malaria in the jungle." He paused, taking a deep breath.

"We left our base camp to make the trip into the forest that day and on to Puerto del Oro. Sandra had the malaria medication she'd gotten in Lima. As we neared the mining camp, I fell behind to talk to one of the mining supervisors. Sandra went ahead so she could administer the drugs to the ill workers."

Erika brushed her hand over his. "Go on."

"After a while, I left to follow her into the village, but … "

The memories must've stung. She gripped his hand to give him support.

"A dispute had arisen over the rights to a gold-digging pit. One of the other missionaries told me later."

Erika's insides churned like an old-fashioned butter maker. His story wouldn't be a happy one.

"There was yelling and then gunshots."

Grief swelled in Erika's heart and traveled up her throat. Before he said another word, she knew what had happened. She clutched her throat. "Oh, no."

"I raced ahead." He struggled to breathe and brushed his hand over his eyes. "She'd gotten caught in the crossfire of the gunshots. She lay in the dirt— motionless. I rushed to her, but she was already gone." His voice broke. "I couldn't save her." He held his hands over his face as his shoulders shook. "Ever since I've blamed myself. I should've been there to protect her."

Erika's voice shook. "I'm so, so sorry, Peyton. No one should have to go through something like that." Before today, she never would've guessed what Peyton would tell her. Now, she could barely endure listening to his story. Her stomach was as tight as the lid on a jar of sour pickles. How could she console him? Nothing would ever change the past.

Peyton's voice squeaked. "I'm afraid that's not the

whole story. There was something else."

Peyton clenched his jaws. Erika deserved to hear the end of the story. "I not only lost my wife; I lost my child. We'd only found out a few days before she was expecting our first baby." Saying the words was painful yet sharing the tragedy with Erika began the process of healing. *Bear each other's burdens.* She did that for him.

Though he'd displayed deep emotions in her presence, he trusted her. He glanced at her face as she brushed tears away.

"I can't imagine carrying that kind of memory. No wonder you had a nightmare tonight." She slipped her arms around his neck and tugged him into a hug. "That's why you came to the ranch, to leave it all behind."

"Yes. No one on the ranch knew me or what happened in my past. As far as anyone else was concerned, I'd never been married or lost a baby. And if I told others, they would only pity me. I couldn't live with that constant reminder. The Ford ranch has been a new start. If only the nightmares would stop. Sometimes I feel like a soldier with PTSD."

She folded her hands in her lap. "May I ask a rather personal question."

"That's fine. I have nothing to hide from you." Being transparent with her began to come easy.

"I've read that healing comes with forgiveness. I want that for you, Peyton."

"I think I know where you're going with this."

She steepled her hands. "Have you been able to forgive those gold miners?"

Peyton focused on Erika in a way he hadn't before. As if she'd doused him with icy water, he caught his breath with the realization. "Perhaps not. At least not in my heart."

If he was finally able to let go of that lifechanging day, would he be free of the nightmares that plagued him? But that wasn't the only reason. He'd needed forgiveness so frequently. Was it time for him to release his animosity toward those people who killed his wife in the Peruvian jungle? He reached for both of Erika's hands, and then he bowed his head. "God, I choose to forgive."

Did Erika dare speak the next question she wanted to ask Peyton? She mustered her courage. "If you'd like to talk about the past, I'm willing to listen if you think it would help." In the soft moonlight, Erika could make out the tension in Peyton's eyes. Reliving Sandra's death hadn't been easy nor would it ever be.

Peyton slowly nodded his head. "I met Sandra in college. We belonged to the same church. After dating a year, we got married. Both of us felt a call to the mission field. I thought we'd live and raise a family somewhere on foreign land. I couldn't have ever imagined that things would end as they did." Peyton took a breath and gripped both of her hands.

"After Sandra died, the mission board offered me a

six-month sabbatical and then asked if I would return but this time work in the city of Lima."

"So, what happened?" He obviously hadn't returned to South America.

He squeezed his eyes shut for a moment and then opened them. "I told the mission board that I wouldn't be returning then. Or perhaps ever. I explained that I wanted to serve God in another way."

"When you first came to the ranch, I knew something was different about you. The way you showed love to Chet and then how willing you were to help Dad with the ranch. Your actions show your love for others." Erika shut her mouth. She hadn't expected to say all that.

Peyton held up his palms. "Wait a minute. Your words are kind, but I can't claim sainthood. I have faults like everyone else."

She laughed. "How long do you plan on staying here?"

Peyton's lips held a smile. "After meeting Chet and Pete, I believe I'd like to operate a ranch for boys like them which would house fewer guys than the home in Oakville—an environment they could call home." He stared straight ahead into the dark night. "When I worked in the corporate world, I made some investments so Sandra and I would be able to purchase a home. I'm thinking of buying a ranch near here."

A bolt of electricity sparked up her spine. "I believe you will someday." She only mouthed the words, "What if I became a part of your plans?"

Peyton missed the feel of Erika's soft hand as she leaned against the swing's cushioned back. Yet, something else filled not his hand but his heart and mind.

But was it too soon? Sandra had been gone over a year now. Though he still loved and missed her, God had more for him. A new life waited. Perhaps a life with Erika. Peace traveled through him bringing hope for the future.

More than ever, the desire to help homeless kids had begun to press upon his mind. Two life-changing decisions were waiting to be accomplish—and soon.

The first sparked a question. "Erika, what are you doing tomorrow? Would you go with me to the realty office in Oakville? I'd like to scout out the market for ranch property in the area. And then go to the bank to check out financing."

Chapter Twenty-Six

Mr. Chambers opened the door to the farmhouse with a master key. "I'll let you look at the place on your own, and then we'll drive around the property to view the barns and the rest of the acreage."

With a wide smile, Peyton swept his hand in front of him and bowed as Erika walked in before him.

She stepped into the wide expanse of the great room. "Third house we've looked at today, and you know what they say." She laughed. "The third time's a charm." She twirled around. "From the outside, this home certainly looks large enough to house a bunch of boys."

"True. And this is the only one with ranch land. The other two wouldn't work for my plan of opening a boys' home in the country."

Erika ginned. "Well, maybe you've found your property."

A sudden rush of exhilaration lingered in Peyton's heart. Did he dare hope that Erika would be a part of his future? He followed her around the house, four bedrooms on the back against a wide, enclosed porch, a master and huge, country kitchen up front. The four bedrooms upstairs made this place perfect for his ministry. He smiled. Whoever built this house must've had a lot of kids or plenty of other family members.

"One thing I love is the wood-burning fireplace and space for a long dining table," Erika said. "I can picture a family here, playing board games and cards, or relaxing and chatting about their day."

Maybe they'd want a large table for a lot of their own kids someday—a notion that dizzied him. "You approve?"

Her eyes sparkled as she stepped nearer. "The house with its cozy and relaxed spaces will be perfect for you." She drew even closer. "But the price, Peyton. Can you afford this place? The pasture and grounds will take a lot of work, too."

"Already taken care of." Peyton smiled. "My investments plus a small loan will cover it."

"It seems God has made a way."

Joy rioted in Peyton's heart. He moved closer and lifted her chin with two fingers. "I hope it will be perfect for you, too. I'm dreaming that you'll be by my side someday."

Erika gazed at Peyton's luminous eyes and kissable lips. Lost in in delirious wonder, she yielded her lips to his. Did she dare dream of a life with Peyton? She slid her fingers through the short strands of his hair as reality faded. All she knew was his strong arms surrounding her and the possibility of a future together.

When finally, he moved his mouth from hers, he trailed his finger along her cheek and then brought his lips to her ear. "I love you, Erika Ford."

She sighed. What would married life be like with this man, living on a ranch with a houseful of boys?

Chapter Twenty-Seven

Friday, Peyton rose from his chair in the small office and pumped the real-estate agent's hand up and down. "Thank you, Mr. Chambers."

The agent returned the handshake. "I'm impressed by your plans for the ranch." Mr. Chamber' gaze met Peyton's. "To devote your life to serving needy boys is admirable."

"The decision has come after much thought and prayer." Peyton took a few steps toward the door.

"I'd say that pretty lady with you helped you decide."

Peyton grinned. He liked the sound of a pretty lady by his side. "Yes, she did, and I'm praying that she'll be a big part of the plan."

Mr. Chambers gathered the paperwork and slid the documents in a manilla folder. "Your earnest money will hold the purchase during the process. We should be able to close in a month—maybe six weeks."

As if Peyton had put on climbing gear, hiked Guadalupe Peak in western Texas, and ascended to the summit, he couldn't feel any more invigorated. Yes, he'd served as a missionary in a foreign land, but now God had placed him in a new location.

Mesquite trees and the greening countryside whizzed past as his truck neared the turnoff to the ranch. On the property before the Ford's, cows meandered across the grassland, now green after the last rain. Would he bring milk producing animals on his ranch or like Erika's family, only raise sheep?

His heart pounded as he pulled into the Ford's long driveway. He had an important question to ask Mr. Ford, but would he say yes?

Peyton parked in front of the bunkhouse and glanced toward the ranch office. Mr. Ford's truck sat to one side.

Peyton's mouth became dry as stale bread as he took a few steps toward the side door. He cleared his throat, tapped on the doorframe, and stepped inside.

At his desk, Mr. Ford pored over some papers sitting on top of a file folder. The older man glanced up and smiled. "Come in, Peyton. I had some figures I wanted to go over with you."

Would he be so receptive when he discovered what Peyton needed to talk about?

Mr. Ford stuck his pencil behind his ear. "I have good news. The ranch is no longer in debt and is making a solid profit, in great part thanks to you."

Peyton paused to savor the moment. "That's amazing."

"Son, if you're willing, I'd like to offer you a full-time position as business manager here at the ranch. Jace has plans to purchase his own ranch in the next year. Austin said he wanted to continue getting his hands dirty shearing sheep and mucking out stables. Who knows about that boy? I think he needs more time to figure things out." He stared at Peyton, probably trying to see how the offer set with him.

Peyton edged into the chair across from the desk. What would Erika's father say when he discovered Peyton had different plans? "I need to speak to you about that subject—a change in my job."

Mr. Ford cocked his head. "All right. Go ahead."

"First, thank you for your offer. It's an honor you would consider me." Peyton swallowed hard. "But something came up in the last few months. It began when Chet and then Pete showed up at the ranch."

Mr. Ford leaned back in his chair. "I'd like to hear what you have to say."

Peyton couldn't procrastinate any longer. Though he didn't want to let Mr. Ford down, he had to follow what God was nudging him to do. "I made a trip to the realty office in Oakville and left earnest money on a contract to purchase ranch land. In fact, it's the ranch directly to the west of the Ford ranch."

Mr. Ford met Peyton's gaze. "The Grimball place. Good land. Grimball took care of it. All those kids of his, and he passed without an heir who wanted to follow after him. This is for that boy's home you mentioned?"

"Yes, sir. If all goes well, I'll close in a little over a month. I realize I'm leaving you without a ranch hand temporarily, but I need to offer my four-week resignation."

Mr. Ford frowned. "About the ranch hand vacancy, I can always put an ad in a publication as before. But as for a ranch manager, I don't believe I can find someone with your ability to fill the spot. I'd like to talk you out of this."

"The first time I met Chet, I understood the pain the

young kid went through. Struggling to take care of himself not to mention his little brother. Then your story about when you were young and the boy you and your family befriended—how he overcame his circumstances—how can I turn my back on these boys? I feel compelled to help them."

Mr. Ford steepled his hands in front of him on the desk. "I don't want to lose you at the ranch." He smiled. "But you won't be far away."

The tightly wound knot in Peyton's stomach began to unravel. He had his boss's approval. But would he agree to Peyton's next question.

Peyton rubbed his fourth finger on his left hand that once wore a gold band. The day he'd removed the ring, he'd finally acknowledged that his marriage had ended. He'd believed no other would replace it. But now ... "There's something else I need to discuss. I shared with Erika about my past. I want to tell you as well."

"All right." Mr. Ford's tone was quiet, expectant as he folded his hands on his desk.

Peyton cleared his voice. "You see, before coming here, I served as a missionary in the jungles of Peru—along with my wife."

Mr. Ford frowned, twirling his pencil in his fingers. "Your wife?"

"Yes, I married a woman I knew from the young adults' group at my church in Dallas. We'd only been married six months. We accepted an assignment from our mission board for the southern jungle." He breathed deeply, relaying the rest of the story.

The older man lowered his voice. "I can't imagine how I would feel if that had happened to me—to watch my wife ... " He scrubbed his hand over his mouth. "I hope living and working at the ranch has been a time of healing."

"Yes, it has." Peyton stared at his hands folded at his waist and then peered into the man's eyes. "But now, my life has changed, and I've moved on. You see, sir…" Peyton gulped. "I've fallen in love with your daughter. She's a blessing from God. I'd like to ask your permission to marry her." He let out a long breath.

Yes, I'd be proud for you to be my son-in-law. No doubt, Peyton would have Mr. Ford's full approval.

Mr. Ford stood at his desk and ran a hand through his hair. He frowned and then lightly tapped his fist on the surface. "I'm sorry but that's not something I can give you right now." Erika's father walked toward the door and out into the bright summer June day.

Chapter Twenty-Eight

The next day, riding the fence line in the north pasture didn't sooth Peyton's thrashing stomach. Why was Mr. Ford so against Peyton marrying his daughter? He hadn't given Peyton the chance to ask Erika.

Perhaps the rancher wanted her to make a life with someone from Oakville, or a man who owned and operated a lucrative, money-making ranch in their county. He nudged Jack's sides to trot on.

One hundred yards ahead, a rider in jeans and a dark blue Stetson, road astride an appaloosa. Since Jace and Austin had gone into town to purchase feed and Mac and Chet were making repairs to the equipment shed, the person couldn't be any of the hands. Perhaps an intruder on the ranch?

Peyton coaxed Jack to trot faster as he approached the horseman.

As he neared, he saw someone—long, blond hair flowing from under a hat.

Erika.

He tapped his forehead. Of course. She was to ride the fence line today to inspect for damage.

He nudged Jack closer and then froze, holding his

breath.

A few feet from Paint, a rattler coiled, ready to strike.

He couldn't yell. The sound would only alarm Paint. Peyton squeezed Jack's sides with his calves and heels to compel him into a run.

Now, not more than ten yards away, his fear became a reality.

Paint reared, giving a loud whinny.

Erika grabbled to hold to Paint's reins. Her fingers slipped from the leather straps, and she slid from the saddle. With a thump, she fell atop a wide, green bush, and rolled a few feet.

Paint's hooves met the ground as he reared again and lowered not more than a few inches from Erika. Then he took off in a sprint in the direction of the ranch.

The snake slithered away toward the west pasture.

No, not again. Peyton bit his cheek. Had Mr. Ford's fear come true? Would he lose his daughter in the same way he lost his sister? Peyton slid off the horse and raced toward Erika, lying motionless on the ground.

"Oh, Erika." Peyton kneeled beside her and touched her cheek. "Can you hear me?"

Long lashes fluttered open, and she frowned. "Peyton," she whispered.

Love stirred within his heart—and emotions he hadn't felt for over a year. More important than anything, he needed to get her help. "Does anything hurt? Are you okay?"

A slight smile worked its way onto Erika's lips. "I guess I passed the test. I'm a full fledge ranch hand now." She groaned and slowly sat up, brushing dust and grass from her arms.

He closed his eyes and took a calming breath. She was okay. Against his better judgement, he wrapped his arms around her, holding her close. "The thought that something might've happened to you—I couldn't have endured it." He smiled with the realization. "I'm in love with you."

She pulled away, and her gaze traveled over his face. "I love you, too."

She loved him? Words he'd longed to hear, words which opened the door for a life together. Now, if only her father would approve …

Though they sat on the dirt road which followed the fence, likely the most unromantic place on the ranch, Peyton traced the line of her smooth lips with his eyes and leaned closer, ready to put his heart out there again. He touched her lips with his.

Erika's arms around him confirmed what he knew. She cared for him as well. But then a lump formed in his stomach and turned rock hard. Though she confirmed her love for him, and he loved her too, none of that mattered. Would Mr. Ford ever give them his approval.

Both pain and pleasure dueled for Erika's attention. Her backside delivered stabs of pain as she gripped Peyton's hand and rose to her feet. Yet, the strong pressure of his arm supporting hers sent a flutter like a flag rippling in the wind.

She balanced her weight on one leg and then the

other. She'd likely be sore tomorrow, but nothing had broken.

She dared to remember Peyton's lips on hers and her wish to remain in his arms forever. The truth exploded inside, she wanted him—and he wanted her, too.

Erika took a few steps forward. Walking back to the ranch might be a challenge right now.

Peyton held her hand and leaned closer, his brows drawn together. "Do you think you can ride Jack to the ranch?"

She nudged his shoulder. "Only if you'll ride behind me."

A grin crept along his lips. "I think I can arrange that."

Erika lifted her knee to place her foot in the saddle's strap, trying to ignore the discomfort in her back.

From behind, Peyton boosted her up so she could swing her other foot over. "Ouch." Sitting in the saddle would be uncomfortable but riding would be better than walking.

The warmth of Peyton's chest behind her eased the jolts as Jack transported them nearer the ranch. She welcomed Peyton's strong arms around her waist, relishing the security and safety they brought.

About a hundred yards away, Erika caught sight of her father on one of the horses.

He spurred his horse into a gallop and then slowed as he neared. "Erika, Paint returned to the ranch without you. I panicked, thinking something had happened to you." He glanced at Peyton.

"Sir, a rattlesnake scared Paint, and he bucked. She fell off Paint."

Mr. Ford gulped a quick breath and squeezed his

eyes shut. "Not like before. No, my girl's okay."

"Yes, Dad, I'm fine. Peyton saw the snake and arrived in time to help me onto Jack."

He peered at Peyton and paused, as if differentiating the past from the present. "Thank you for coming to my daughter's rescue. The same horrible accident didn't happen again, praise God." He turned the reins on his horse to head back. "I've done some thinking, Peyton. After we see to Erika, can we talk in my office?"

Erika shifted in the saddle. Was Dad going to fire Peyton?

"Are you sure you're okay?" Peyton murmured into Erika's ear as they neared the ranch, the faint scent of lavender enticing him to seek another kiss.

"Yes, only sore."

He had no choice but to believe her, and he wanted to be certain she was. He slid off the horse and held out his arms, supporting Erika's waist as she dismounted.

On the ground, she turned to him, longing in her eyes.

He grasped her fingers and kissed the back of her hand. "I'm so grateful you're okay."

She placed her index finger on her lips, touched his, and then hobbled toward the house. "I need a cup of peppermint tea and a hot bath with Epson salts."

He nodded to her with a grin. "You earned it." Since Peyton had seen Erika's father walk into his office, he figured the rancher was ready to talk.

Doubt held him like a vice. Peyton turned toward

the outside office door. Like he'd eaten a full meal of spicy food, his stomach soured. Since he'd turned down Peyton's request to marry his daughter, perhaps Mr. Ford had decided to order him out of his daughter's life. Maybe he somehow blamed Peyton for Erika's accident today.

Peyton turned the doorknob with his sweaty hand and walked in.

Mr. Ford pointed to the chair, no smile on his face.

As if he sat on thorns, Peyton shuffled on the hard surface. "Mr. Ford, Erika's accident was terrible—"

Mr. Ford lifted his hand in a stop position. "Discovering that Erika's horse threw her felt as if the past repeated itself, but I realize none of it was your fault. And I also figured out something else. I acted like a cantankerous, grumpy, and stiff-necked old man when you asked for her hand in marriage. I want to apologize. I'm still trying to hold on to my Erika, afraid to lose her."

"Sir—"

"I've allowed fear to control me. And it almost did, but God spared my precious Erika. You've been nothing but helpful on this ranch. You're an upstanding, honest, and godly young man. I'd be more than happy to have you as a son-in-law."

Peyton resisted the urge to hug the man. Mr. Ford had given his blessing, and he was free to propose to Erika. "Then do I have permission to ask her—"

"Yes, yes. I'd like nothing more. Mrs. Ford and myself have discussed the matter. We think you'd make a fine husband for our daughter."

Joy rioted in his chest. Peyton rose to shake Mr. Ford's hand. Erika loved him, her father had given his permission, and he placed the down payment on a ranch. What could possibly go wrong now?

Chapter Twenty-Nine

Peyton swiped the razor along his cheeks and rinsed the cream and whiskers down the drain. He pulled a comb through his hair and splashed a few drops of aftershave on his neck. He chuckled. What did it matter? The sheep didn't care how he smelled this morning.

Four weeks had passed since Erika's father had given his permission. Was Peyton's decision to wait until the day he signed for the ranch to propose a good one? In any case, the signing day had arrived, and Peyton was free to ask Erika to be his wife.

A swarm of grasshoppers bounced around in his stomach. Besides signing the final contract today, he still had to figure out a memorable way to ask for her hand.

He glanced at his phone. He had plenty of time to get to his appointment at the title company later this afternoon.

So far, no special idea had come to his mind for a proposal. What about in Sadie's stall where they first met? He wrinkled his brow. Not the most charming of locations. What if he took her to the new property and proposed on the front lawn? Hm. He was as romantic as most guys. He could make it work. He chuckled and plopped down on his bed to pull on his boots.

Peyton hauled his ringing phone from his pocket and glanced at the screen. "Hey, Dad. "How's it going?"

Silence filled the phone, and then he heard a low whimper.

Peyton's stomach twisted into a ball. This couldn't be good. "Dad, what is it?"

"Son." Dad's voice was strained and weak. "I need for you to come home."

No doubt Dad was sick or had injured a limb. "Are you okay?"

"No." Dad cleared his throat. "It's your mom. We lost her last night."

"What?" Peyton gripped his fingers into tight fists. He could barely comprehend Dad's words. "What … happened?" Now his stomach turned to gall.

"She left for the store. She'd forgotten to get carrots for her pot roast dinner." A sob choked Dad's voice. "Son, she never made it back."

As if in a bad dream, Peyton didn't want to believe his father's words. He groaned, placing his head in his hands. *No, Lord.*

"The police said someone high on alcohol hit her head-on. Thank God she didn't suffer." Dad spoke, his speech heavy with tension.

Peyton gritted his teeth. If only the driver would suffer a swift execution in the courts of justice. Then he took a breath. *God, deal with this one according to Your will.* It wasn't Peyton's place to seek revenge though he'd grieve for his mother for the rest of his life.

Peyton plastered the phone to his ear. His sweet mother. He couldn't believe he'd never see her again.

"I need you with me. The arrangements for the funeral, I don't want to do this alone."

His heart ached and his plans seemed to crumble beneath him. "Of course, Dad. I'll leave in a few minutes and will be there by this evening."

"I love you, Peyton." The waver in Dad's voice tripped him up, and he couldn't restrain the moisture in his eyes.

As if sleepwalking, Peyton made his way out of the bunkhouse. Find Erika. He had to speak to her.

Inside the big house in the dining room, Erika sat at the main table in front of a plate of scrambled eggs and sipped her morning coffee. She glanced up with a smile and then her grin faded.

"May I speak to you?" Grief began to absorb him. He could barely restrain the tears.

Erika followed him into the den. She turned to grip his hands. "Something isn't right."

Peyton fought the emotion that tried to steal his words as he told her about his father's call. He balled his fists. "Death has claimed too many people. I'm not sure how much more … " He shouldn't think of Sandra at a time like this, but he did.

When he'd be able to return, he didn't know. He tried to memorize the feel of Erika's soft arms around his neck. "Can you please explain to your father for me? I love you, Erika."

A week later, Erika drew her arms around herself as she looked out at the sun slowly disappearing on the horizon. How she longed to be with Peyton during this painful time, but it simply didn't work. Dad needed her on the ranch. Also, a stranger might make Peyton's family uncomfortable.

How many would come for the funeral? Peyton had spoken of a sister. Uncertainty crept along her spine. She knew very little about his family.

Peyton had come from a different lifestyle than hers. A family who enjoyed big-city life might not understand ranching, but he'd adopted so quickly to the routine around here. Falling in love with him had been no mistake

Doubts continued to trouble her. How long would he need to remain with his father? Peyton loved ranching. Hadn't he made plans for the property he'd intended to buy?

She shook her head. What had happened to the upcoming contract he was to sign? He hadn't mentioned anything before he'd left. Erika sank into the lawn chair. "God, I'm not sure what's going on with Peyton, but I pray he'll find peace and closure."

Her phone rang. She looked at the screen. Peyton. A glint of hope accelerated her pulse. "Hello, Peyton. I'm glad to hear from you." She rose and paced the grass in front of her.

"I'm sorry I haven't called sooner." He spoke the words slowly and with deliberation. "Dad and I had to make arrangements and then the funeral … "

Erika's heart pounded. "It's okay. I've prayed for you every day."

"Thank you." He cleared his throat. "I've never seen my father like this before. He's lost without my mom. He's indecisive, only wanting to sit in his easy chair for most of the day. He probably wouldn't eat if I didn't fix him a meal. I never expected this. I'm not sure when I can return."

"I'll explain everything to Dad. I'm sure he'll understand." She gained a sudden gleam of insight. "For so long, I tried to put life in a box, believing that I could control everything. I'm beginning to learn that some things are unpredictable."

"There's something else, Erika. The day I left, I was to finalize the papers for the purchase of the ranch. I called on my way to Dallas and canceled the appointment, explaining the circumstances."

"But couldn't your broker or the mortgage company send the documents to you via e-mail?"

"Yes, but I waited. I wanted to make sure my father was stable, that he could handle life on his own."

"Sure, I get it. Your first obligation is to family." How could she deny that?

"Yes, but the decision to wait was one of the hardest I've ever made though I still think it was for the best. Now I'm afraid I've lost my earnest money and the contract."

"If there's anything I can do … "

"I can't predict the future. I don't know how this is going to end."

"I understand." But did she? There was the possibility that Peyton wouldn't return to the ranch. And if he didn't, she'd have to figure out a way to do life without him. How was she supposed to when he'd stolen her heart and taken it with him?

Chapter Thirty

Perspiration rolled from Erika's brow into her eyes. She glanced overhead at the morning sun as she wiped the moisture away. Guess she'd have to weed the garden at 7:00 a.m. instead of nine next time.

Her gaze traveled to the bunkhouse. Any moment Peyton would amble out, his wide shoulders swaying with each step. Then sadness coursed through her veins threatening to travel to her heart. Peyton wasn't here, and she didn't know when he'd return. Nothing to do but put his absence out of her mind. But how was she supposed to accomplish the feat when every beat of her heart spoke his name?

The two weeks since his call to say he didn't know when he'd return seemed like two years. Her heart clenched. She couldn't imagine losing a spouse and then a parent within such a short time period. Witnessing Peyton's love and support for his father reinforced her admiration for the guy.

Erika retrieved the bucket filled with weeds and dumped the contents in the ranch burn pile behind Jace and Charlotte's house. She shielded her eyes from the bright sun as she glanced toward the west.

Her father's land extended ten miles or so to the

next property—the ranch Peyton wanted to purchase. The land on which he'd placed the earnest money. Based on her last conversation with him, he hadn't finalized the contract. She closed her eyes, and the notion struck with the force of a tornado. Marching toward the house, she set the empty bucket next to the garage. A quick change of clothes before she headed into town.

Erika gripped the folder the agent at the realty office had given her, the documents inside. A stab of doubt tugged at her heart. Had she done the right thing? The agent hadn't spoken with the confidence she hoped for.

"I should let you know in a couple of days if the title company will accept the offer. We'll have to verify the funds and do a background check."

Surprise and the temptation to raise her voice almost overcame her. "What do you mean background check? I've lived here at the Ford ranch all my life. Besides, I'm offering a large downpayment."

The agent drew a hand through his hair. "I realize that, Erika, but it's standard procedure when processing a loan."

The agent wasn't to blame. Erika blew out a long stream of air and turned toward the door. "All right, then. I'll wait for your instructions."

"I'll be in touch."

Would she accomplish her goal or had she wasted her time?

Chapter Thirty-One

Thunder cracked and lightning flashed across the sky with the rare July storm. Peyton stood at the window of his childhood home in Dallas and gazed at the display. After ten minutes, he shifted away and turned to Dad settled in his easy chair.

For days Peyton had tried to get his father out of the house, and he'd always made up an excuse why he couldn't. Dad hadn't attended church though in the past he and Mom had never missed a Sunday without good reason. Would this coming Sunday be any different? "I don't think the rain will keep up all day. I'd hoped we could go fishing later on."

His parent glanced up with a look that said he heard what Peyton said, but he shook his head. "Don't think I'm up to getting out on the lake today."

His father, at least ten pounds lighter since Peyton had returned home, concerned him. He'd never seen him act so depressed. Even the visit from Peyton's sister during the funeral hadn't perked him up. Though Peyton longed to return to the Ford ranch, how could he leave him now?

Peyton set his coffee cup on the side table and pulled up the footstool in front of the recliner. "I didn't mention this before the funeral, but I'd like to tell you about some plans I want to make. Maybe you'd even be interested in coming with me."

Dad lifted weary eyes. "I'm sorry. I've been thinking about your mom for so long, I never asked how things were going at the Ford ranch." He shook his head and gazed at his lap. "And I didn't think about how you lost someone as well. You lost the woman who gave you birth." Dad sighed, probably reminding himself of the truth as well.

"It's been tough on all of us, but we will heal." Tough was the understatement. Peyton wouldn't mention that he'd lost his wife same as Dad had. He patted his father's shoulder. "I have an idea. I want to open a place for boys without stable homes, who suffer abuse, and whose parents aren't around to give them guidance. The open range and fresh air of a ranch could bring healing and the chance to start a new life." Now that he thought of it, that life would do Dad some good, too. But would he ever want to join him?

Dad sat forward in the chair, the first spark of interest Peyton had seen since he'd returned home. "How did that idea come about?"

"I met two brothers at the ranch who need a home. Their story intrigued me, and something within said I needed to help them and other boys like them." Each time he relayed the story, his enthusiasm deepened.

"You've always wanted to live your life helping others." Dad sat back in the chair and smiled. "I remember when you were little, we had an elderly neighbor. You used to carry in her groceries or set her newspaper on her porch. No surprise you went to Peru." Dad muttered as he stared at his feet. "Now that I think of it, your mom was the second family member you've lost."

Peyton hadn't expected Dad to recognize Sandra's death at that moment. "It's been over a year." But Peyton had found a measure of healing now. Hopefully his father would experience the same.

Crash. Boom.

Peyton flinched. The old panic rose in his chest, and he jerked his gaze around the room. No, Dallas was merely experiencing a thunder storm. He took a long breath and paced the living room. In a few more minutes, his pounding heart returned to normal. But had the symptoms completely disappeared from his life, or would the nightmares continue?

He forced the thoughts away. "While I was at the ranch, I put earnest money down on a property I hoped to purchase, but I dropped everything when I came home again. Later I found a text on my phone dated July seventh. I'd totally missed reading it."

"What did the message say?" Dad's interest seemed to perk up.

"That I'd lose the contract if I didn't sign by the next day. It was a week later when I opened the message." Peyton rose from his seat. "I'll be honest. I haven't called the realty office since then."

Dad ran his hand through his hair. "I'm sorry, Peyton. I feel partially responsible."

"No, absolutely not. The problem was my own. I'm curious, however, if the ranch is still on the market. Excuse me, Dad." It was a long shot, but he could always call.

Peyton dialed the number and walked to his bedroom. After asking for his realter, he waited.

Whatever happened was in God's hands now. "This is Peyton Langley, Mr. Chambers."

"Yes, Peyton. How are you doing?"

"I realize how long I took to get back you. I've been dealing with a serious family situation for the last several weeks. Is the land I was to purchase on the market now?"

"Mr. Langley, as I said when I left you my message, you had to forfeit your earnest money and the contract if we didn't hear from you. I'm terribly sorry, but the property went back on the market and has now sold."

"I understand. I'm at fault here. You see my mother … " Why bother offering an excuse now? Though the realtor's words didn't surprise him, the truth was hard to hear. "Are there any comparable listings for sale in the area?"

"I'm sorry. Not at this time. Ranch property doesn't come up for sale every day, but you never know. I can put you on a waiting list."

"Yes, please do." But what were the chances for a new listing?

Peyton's hope of a ministry to boys had blown up like fireworks on the Fourth of July. Though he loved Erika, should he return to Oakville and the ranch now since he'd lost the property he was to purchase? He could take her dad up on his job offer, but he feared every day he'd regret settling for something other than his dream. And who knew when another ranch would be for sale?

His most important obligation now was to see his father recover from the unexpected loss of Peyton's mother and to see his father return to a normal life. But would that happen in the foreseeable future?

Chapter Thirty-Two

In the sheep barn, Erika patted Sam's head. "You know, fellow, it's been two weeks since I talked to the real-estate agent."

Sam cocked his head to one side as if he pondered her words.

Her stomach churned as she glanced at the screen. "Sam, you must've worked your magic. This is the agent. Hello."

"Miss Ford." The real estate agent's voice met her ears. "I'm happy to say your loan has been approved. Can you come in later this afternoon to finalize papers?"

She swung her other hand in a fist pump. "I definitely can. See you then." She gave Sam's head another pat. "That was good news."

Two weeks after Peyton talked to the agent, he strolled to the living room window. Bleating and baaing of sheep played in his memory and his heart, stirring desire for a life with Erika and regret he'd lost his dream of a boys' ranch. *Admit it.* He longed to return to the Ford place, Erika, and the plans he'd made, but that door had slammed hard in his face. And he'd never abandon his father if he needed him.

Dad sat in his usual spot facing the TV—the easy chair. He clicked off the television and glanced at Peyton.

Could the spark he'd seen in Dad's eyes this morning at breakfast mean that his father was returning to his old self? Peyton whispered another prayer under his breath.

"Son." Dad rose from his easy chair. "You wanta go to the stables today? I'm thinking a horseback ride would do me some good."

Peyton raised his brow. Dad suggesting an activity that took them out of the house? Unbelievable. "Yeah, sure, Dad. Great idea. I haven't been on the back of a horse since I left the ranch."

"I haven't gone riding since your mom died." Dad winced. "I need to ask for your forgiveness."

Like a phantom returning from another world, the thoughtful, kind parent Peyton had always known seemed to have come home. Peyton neared his father and gripped his shoulder. "You've done nothing for me to forgive."

Dad turned to face him. "I couldn't have asked for a better son. You dropped everything when your mom left us. I didn't bounce back like I thought I would."

"You're my father. I remember the times when you showed me patience—especially when Sandra died." Though the memories were still there, the pain of missing her no longer pulverized his heart as in the past. "I love you."

His father lifted his gaze to the window and the glorious sunny day, the lawn Peyton had recently mowed and the August flowers displaying their colors in the beds and along the back fence. He grinned. "Tell me more about that ranch you want to buy."

As if Peyton was a boy and his father had announced that Santa was arriving, his heart rose to his throat. Dad was making progress. But more than that, a green flag waved in his mind's eye. Perhaps he could find a way to fulfill his dream after all. If there was no ranch land for sale, he could always work for Mr. Ford with the understanding he would move on when a listing came up. Who knew, maybe a new ranch property wouldn't take long to pop up on the Oakville MLS.

Peyton dropped to the couch and nodded for Dad to sit down. "I have photos of the land I'd wanted to buy. It's no longer for sale, but I'm willing to wait for others." He scrolled through the pictures of the property for which he'd placed the earnest money.

"Tell me more about your plans." Dad propped his ankle over his knee.

For the next thirty minutes Peyton explained his vision for a boys' ranch and his relationship with Erika. If he emphasized how he lost the ranch, he might add more grief to Dad's mental state. Best to gloss over that for now.

A twinkle glistened in Dad's eyes. The confident, easygoing father he'd always known had emerged from his grief. "You explained how you'd serve as a father figure to the children you take in. What would you think about adding a grandfather figure?"

Erika sipped her peach tea and soaked up the last rays as the sun dipped below the hills. The evening breeze cooled her after the hot day, typical for the middle of August in central Texas.

She peered at her cell phone and reached for it. Then she replaced it on the table beside her, something she'd done a thousand times since Peyton had left two months ago, today. She still couldn't wrap her brain around it.

A little more than eight weeks ago, she and Peyton had looked at the land he wanted to buy, the location of his future and his dreams. But she'd heard very little from him. She supposed his one phone call and several texts would have to do. Face it. Peyton had another life now and had likely forgotten her and Ford ranch. But what happened to the ministry he'd cherished? Perhaps he'd chosen another way to serve God near Dallas.

Erika set the glass of iced tea on the side table and strolled to the edge of the tiled patio. A mockingbird whistled, as if bringing encouragement. Did Peyton enjoy a bird's warbles and chirps where his father lived?

Her phone dinged, reminding her of her second appointment tomorrow at Oakville Realty. But had she made the right decision? If she didn't carry out her plans, Peyton might never have a chance at his dreams—that is if he ever returned. She rubbed her brow.

The sound of a motor told her that someone had turned up the driveway. Erika rounded the corner of the house by Dad's office and stepped onto the front porch.

The vehicle drew closer and then Erika's mouth dropped open as two men exited the car.

As if in a trance, Erika stood motionless, staring at the scene before her.

The one with brown hair, light brown eyes, and well-defined muscles neared, shapely lips slightly parted. "Hello, Erika. I didn't call. I guess I was afraid you'd hang up on me."

The other man who looked like Peyton but older, a slight smile on his face, waved.

Words lodged in her throat. "I don't know what to say." She never expected him to walk up to her front door—no notice or explanation. If she wasn't so happy to see him, she'd be angry. Did he expect her to welcome him, no questions asked?

He took two steps toward her, and she took two back.

He held both palms up. "Erika, my life's been so crazy lately. I hope you're not going to walk in the house and slam the door in my face."

Now a flush of anger steamed her insides. Yes, she wanted to see him, but after all this time with no explanation? Why hadn't he even bothered to call?

He folded his hands. "I don't blame you if you hate me."

The pathetic, pleading look in Peyton's eyes and on his face began to unravel her proud heart. The guy had lost his mother and cared for his father. "No, I could never hate you." She glanced at the man behind Peyton for a few seconds.

"Please forgive me. There's so much to tell you." Peyton reached to tug the other man closer. "I'd like for you to meet my father."

Chapter Thirty-Three

The befuddled thought forged through Peyton's brain. Could he and Erika span the distance he'd placed between them and find their connection again?

Erika offered Dad a smile as she shook his hand. Though Peyton might not be welcome at the Ford ranch, at least his father was. "We booked a room in Oakville after we stopped by the realty office. But I couldn't wait any longer to get to the ranch."

Erika focused her gaze on him as if asking a silent question and then turned to his father. "I'm glad to see you, Mr. Langston. Come inside to meet my family." She led him up the porch stairs and in through the front door.

Erika's parents along with Jace and Charlotte and Austin lounged in the den in front of the TV. After introductions were made, Mrs. Ford offered key lime pie left from dinner. "We think so much of your son. He told us about his mother passing. We're so sorry for your loss."

Dad nodded. "I appreciate that."

His father was accepted among the Ford clan as Peyton had hoped. His dad's ease in meeting strangers was an indication that he'd progressed in the healing process, for which Peyton was grateful. With Dad settled between Mr. Ford and Jace on the couch, Peyton turned to Erika. "Could we talk in private, please?"

Erika raised her brows and then nodded. "Let's go to

the backyard. The fireflies are showing up every evening."

Once again, Peyton settled into the swing-for-two near the back deck. He didn't blame Erika for sitting as far away on the seat as she could. He saw it now. He'd made a big mistake by not getting in touch, especially after Dad had begun to improve.

Erika rested her hands in her lap. "How's everything with your father?"

"He's finally getting back to his normal self." Peyton slipped his hand over hers.

Erika wiggled her fingers away from under his and leaned against the back cushion. "I can't imagine losing a loved one."

He'd moved too fast. "Can you please forgive me for not calling? I'm not offering an excuse, but I was scared my father wouldn't pull out of his depression. I spent every moment trying to help him, trying to get him to take an interest in life again. After the funeral, he didn't want to go anywhere. He only sat at home clutching Mom's picture. Before, I never would've predicted this, that his grief would run so deep."

She turned to gaze at him. "I've read that grieving can be hard on your health. I can understand why you were concerned."

"I never expected this kind of struggle to happen in our own family. Still, I'm sorry I got so tied up with Dad that too much time passed before I remembered another family and my life at the Ford ranch." He ran his hand through his hair.

For the first time since he'd arrived, Erika looked at him the same way she had before, love in her eyes.

"Not only did I let you down, I lost the ranch I'd

wanted to purchase. I waited too long before finalizing the contract and lost my earnest money. The property went back on the market and sold." He shook his head.

Erika lingered with the truth a few moments, a sense of calm settling into her stomach. Peyton's face wouldn't be filled with disappointment and failure much longer. She touched her finger to his cheek. "Wait, Peyton. I have something to tell you."

"Yeah?" Peyton scratched his head.

"It's about the ranch you wanted to purchase." She anchored her hand at her hip. "You're right. The ranch sold to another buyer."

He reached toward her and paused and then dropped his hand to his side. "What are you trying to say?"

"Another buyer purchased the ranch. Someone you know well."

Peyton stared at her wide-eyed. "Who? Your father?" His brow formed a V.

"No." She pointed a thumb to her chest. "You're looking at her."

He gawked at her in stunned silence and shook his head. "What are you talking about? You bought the property? I can't imagine why."

She held up her hands. "Let me explain." She rather enjoyed his bewildered behavior. "Time passed, and you hadn't returned. I realized you'd lose your earnest money if you didn't complete the contract. It was too late to save your money but not too late to save your dream. My timing was good. I went down to the realty office the first day the ranch went back on the market. Mr. Chambers helped me to get qualified with the bank—who knew that being a Ford held clout—and I purchased it."

Peyton's frown confused her, and her heart ached. Didn't he appreciate what she'd done for him?

"Why?" Peyton's tone was as dry as the west Texas desert.

"This ranch for needy boys was your dream, your intended life's work." Her voice caught with the first syllable, and then anger rose in her throat because of his ungrateful response. "I knew you'd return someday, but the property wouldn't stay on the market long."

Peyton tilted his head to one side. "But the financing … "

"Hey," she poked him in the chest. "You're not the only one who can manage his finances. I've invested my income for years and had enough for a healthy down payment."

As if she'd withheld a military secret from him, he firmed his jaw and peered at her. "You didn't tell me you were interested in purchasing land."

"I haven't been—until now." She huffed. "Don't you understand? I wanted to save the property from getting snatched up by another buyer. If you never came back, I'd at least have an investment."

His lips hardened into a scowl. "That was my dream, not yours."

Erika shook her head in an attempt to clear the ringing in her ears. Had she heard him correctly? She thought he'd be excited to learn she'd saved the ranch for him.

Peyton bolted from the swing. His grimace said it

all. "I need some space."

A flame of heat crept across Erika's cheeks as Peyton disappeared around the corner of the house.

Chapter Thirty-Four

Erika tugged Paint's reins with a little more pressure than necessary to steer the animal back to the ranch. With each bounce atop her horse, confusion threatened to unnerve her.

Four days now and she hadn't heard from Peyton about her purchase of the property—a done deal now. She poked out her lower lip. Unbelievable his last words—and the way he plodded out of the backyard after she told him about the mortgage on his ranch— now hers. She'd only intended to help him while he dealt with his mother's death and family matters. She clenched her jaws until they hurt.

Perhaps he'd deceived her. She'd taken him for a God-fearing, kind man who cared about her. Case in point: the day he'd protected her and Sam in the cellar during the tornado. She shook her head. What had changed?

Dad waved as she and Paint trotted up to the horse barn. She dismounted and led Paint closer to the stables. "Hey, Dad."

Dad swooped off his hat, shooing away a fly, and then plopped his Stetson on again. "What's going on with Peyton? I saw his father in front of the coffee shop downtown. Mr. Langston said Peyton was going through a tough time. He's trying to make some decisions."

"As you already know, Dad, Peyton put earnest money down to purchase the ranch adjacent to ours. He planned to establish a home for boys like Chet and Pete, a place where they could thrive and learn about the Lord." Erika uncinched the straps and pulled the saddle off her horse. "But he headed home when his mother passed."

"Yes, yes. You came to me with the news he'd returned to Dallas—sorry he had to leave so suddenly." Dad frowned and took the saddle from her, hoisting it atop the wood rack. "So, when did he plan to sign the contract on the ranch?"

"Honestly, I think at that point the contract was the last thing on his mind. His father experienced shock and then depression after Peyton's mother died. Peyton was afraid to leave him alone." She rubbed her forehead. "Please keep the information to yourself. If it were my family, I wouldn't want to publicize personal matters."

"Of course, honey. And I can understand his father's state of mind at a time like that." Dad's voice held a hint of sympathy.

"And Peyton's. He told me he didn't contact the realty office and lost his earnest money and the sale."

"Peyton's grief is one thing, but letting the sale go … doesn't sound like the Peyton I know."

Erika pulled the curry comb off the shelf and began to loosen the excess dirt on Paint's coat. "True, but I believe Peyton's concern over his father took precedence, and he thought of nothing else. His situation broke my heart." The notion stung, like that of an angry wasp. "I couldn't stand the thought of his plans coming to nothing."

"I'd say you care a lot about him." Dad unsaddled his horse.

"I do. And as you know, I've built my investment accounts through the years." She stared at the hard brush in her hand. "I did what I thought was a kindness. I put a contract on the house and property."

Dad widened his eyes. "You bought the ranch?"

"Yes, I meant to keep it for Peyton."

"And if he never returned?" Dad's frown didn't help.

"It doesn't hurt to have an additional investment. I could've leased it to a rancher."

"That's true." Dad lifted his saddle over the wood rack next to Erika's.

Erika swiped the brush over Paint's coat. "I never expected Peyton's reaction—as if I'd interfered in his business, and he didn't like it one bit." She glanced away, not wanting to see Dad's expression, critical of what she'd done. "I figured he'd at least be grateful that he didn't lose the ranch."

Dad ground the heel of his boot on the sawdust floor and faced her with a smile. "You want to know the truth? Sometime men can be as stubborn as a stain on a shirt that won't come out. Ask your mom. She can tell you. You likely hurt his ego. Men like to think they're handling things, that they're in charge."

Erika gripped her hands on her waist and tried to strangle the fierce tide of emotions warring within. "That's ridiculous. I only wanted to help. I had his best interests at heart. Why couldn't he see that?"

Dad reached to grip her hands. "I raised three boys, and I'm one myself. I understand where he's coming from. But give him some time. He'll come to his senses."

Erika shrugged and continued to pull the hard brush through Paint's coat. "If you say so." She'd heard that men had a hard time understanding women, but now she was convinced, women had a hard time understand men, too.

But was Dad right? Would Peyton come to his senses?

The greasy hamburger sat half eaten on Peyton's plate. He stared at his father across the table, not really seeing him. His thoughts dwelled in another place—back at the Ford ranch and the last time he saw Erika.

Dad wiped his mouth with the napkin and wadded the paper into a ball, tossing it next to his plate. "Can an older, perhaps wiser man give you some advice?"

Peyton drew his attention to his father and shrugged. Sure, his dad was full of guidance, but it was probably too late to do anything about anything now.

"I think you need to hear the truth." A faint glimpse of amusement crossed his lips. "You love this girl. I can see the way you act around her. Is she worth losing because of your egotistical pride?"

"What?" Peyton flinched and sat up straight, unable to believe his father's words. Egotistical pride?

"I'm sure that sounded harsh, but you need to know the truth." Dad pinned him with a stare. "She only meant well by purchasing the land. She did it because she loves you, too. Do you want to give up this dream of yours?"

Peyton shrank farther down into the seat. Dad's words echoed in his brain, and heat steamed his face. His father was right. He took a sip of water as a flicker of understanding glowed in his heart. "I acted like a jerk." Each word pierced him like a poke of a knife as he spoke.

"You took the first step. Admitting you were wrong." Dad folded his hands over his chest.

Peyton swallowed hard. "You suppose it's too late to apologize?"

His father leaned back in his chair and rested his hands on the back of his head. "If I have my guess, I'd say she's waiting up there at that ranch for you to show up."

Peyton rose from the table. "You wanta take a ride out there with me?"

"Sure. If I'm going to work on one someday, there's no time like the present to start learning how to be a ranch hand." He threw a tip on the table. "Oh, and I suggest you stop at the floral shop to get an elegant bouquet of flowers and chocolates cookies from that bakery I saw."

Peyton guffawed. "Sounds like you're speaking from experience."

Peyton chuckled to himself. He'd supported his father when he needed him, but this time around, Dad was there for him with his wisdom that came from his years on earth.

His father set out for the bunkhouse after Peyton pulled up in front of the ranch house. Peyton exited the car and carefully removed the flower arrangement and the box of cookies. Would this meager offering work in his favor, or would Erika tell him to get lost?

He glanced around, and then he spotted her, standing in the middle of a patch of pumpkin vines and green zucchini, a water hose in her hand.

Erika glanced up from the garden and blinked.

Like an awkward school kid, Peyton drug his feet as he neared her. "These are for you, if you'll take them." He held out the bouquet of flowers.

She stared at him with a blank look. "A peace offering?"

Sweat dropped off Peyton's brow. "Uh … yeah." His muscles tensed as words seemed to freeze on his lips.

The expression on her face didn't change as she reached for the flowers. "They're lovely."

"Do you like chocolate cookies?" He set the box at the edge of the garden.

Erika's cheeks turned rosy as she giggled. "My favorite."

"Will you give me a chance, er, can I explain?" He combed a quick hand through his hair.

She nodded. "I suppose that's fair. Meet me out back where we talked last time." She took the cookies and the flowers in through the front door.

Peyton rung his wet hands together as he edged down on the swing. Why was admitting his pride had gotten in the way such a hard thing to do?

Moments later, the fresh aroma of gardenias settled around him, and Erika relaxed onto the other side of the swing.

"You smell nice." Even out working in the garden in the sunshine, she smelled fresh.

She pushed her foot along the ground to set the swing in motion.

Peyton dared to grasp her hand like an awkward teenager. "I allowed my ego to get the best of me. My dad pointed that out to me."

"You father?" An easy smile covered her lips.

"Yes, my dad. He has a lot of wisdom most of the time." Peyton turned to her and lifted her hand to his lips for a kiss. "I'm sorry."

She didn't pull away. "I only wanted to help you."

His heart sped up like a race car in the Indy 500. "I get that now. I was bullheaded and listened to that conceited voice inside my head that said I had to accomplish my goal on my own terms. Can you forgive me?"

Erika withdrew her hand from his and stared at her lap.

He threw his hands up in the air. "Come on, Erika. I acted like a jerk, but I'm not sure what I'd do without you." He trailed his finger down her cheek. "Please accept my apology."

She lingered a few more minutes, facing straight ahead, and then looked at him, her eyes filled with playfulness. "I do." She whispered.

Peyton pulled her into his arms, wishing he could hold her like this forever. To bask in the fresh scent of her body and touch her soft skin. Erika's words rang in his heart. Would she be willing to say those words again one day before a pastor and God's people?

Chapter Thirty-Five

Erika gripped Peyton's hand as they exited his car. "When can I take off the blindfold?" She felt for his shoulder.

"We're almost there." With a gentle touch, he held her arm and guided her across a grassy surface. "Now, step up. There are three stairs."

Her boots clicked on what she figured was a wooden floor. Since he'd insisted on her wearing the blindfold since they left the ranch, she wasn't sure what direction he'd taken her. A cool breeze brushed against her cheeks, like on the front porch at the ranch.

He nudged her shoulder down and held onto her other arm. "There's a chair for you. Have a seat here."

Erika gripped his arm until she felt the support of what seemed to be a lawn chair, perhaps an Adirondack with its slanted back.

Peyton fiddled with the tie on the blindfold and allowed the cloth to drop into her lap.

The sun sat close to the horizon as pink puffy clouds floated across the darkening sky. She glanced around at the back porch of the Grimball home she'd purchased while he was in Dallas. "Why did you bring me here?" She had a notion of the reason but didn't want to get her hopes up.

Peyton slipped down into the chair beside her. "We need to talk, and I figured the best place would be at the property in question."

Erika peered at his face, trying to understand where he was going with this.

He smoothed his hand over hers. "As you know, I'd like to own and operate a group home for boys someday at this ranch although I let the property slip out of my hands for a while. You, in your kindness, got it back for me."

"Peyton—"

"First, I need to settle some financial matters with you. In the next week, I plan to reimburse you for your downpayment and any monthly payments you've made so far."

She lifted her index finger.

"No, hear me out. I'm not taking no for an answer. Though I'm repaying you for the initial investments, I want the place to be in both our names."

She nodded. If they were to be a team someday, that would be appropriate.

He squeezed her hand. "First, I need to ask you an important question."

She couldn't find her breath as Peyton rose from his chair and knelt before her. She'd dreamed about a life with the handsome rancher, but their romance always seemed to hit a snag. Was now the right time?

Peyton pulled a little box out of his jeans pocket. "I can't get you out of my mind. Your smile makes my heart pound. I'm falling in love with you."

He'd shredded her heart to ribbons when he hadn't trusted her with the purchase of the ranch. Could she trust him this time? A flush of emotion welled up inside and she knew. He'd been man enough to apologize. She was free to surrender her heart to him. "Peyton, I ... "

"I want to spend the rest of my life together. Will you marry me?"

Her lips began to form the word *yes*, but no sound emerged. Like a rain cloud on the horizon, a doubt crept into her mind. What if he couldn't forget Sandra? Could she compete with his wife's memory?

A frown formed on his brow. "Erika, is there something wrong?"

"The past ... what if we get married, and you realize you can't forget your first wife?"

Peyton rose from his knee and poked the box in his pocket again. He got the message. Maybe he hadn't completely thought out everything before he proposed to her. Spending every day and every night with Erika. Living in the same house, making meals together, like he and Sandra used to do, facing financial problems, would he compare her to Sandra? He firmed his lips. No. Absolutely not. He couldn't think of anything more unfair. Besides, he loved Erika for who she was, not as a substitute for Sandra.

From the porch's railing, he relished the beauty before him, one shiny star glimmering in a sky of deep blue. Sure, he'd always love Sandra, but she no longer lived on this earth, and Erika did. Erika was alive and vibrant and beautiful. His heart told him, he couldn't live without her. He swung around.

The chair where Erika sat a few moments ago was empty, the blindfold on the floor. She'd disappeared like the sun behind the horizon. Regret tugged at his heart. "Erika, where'd ya go?"

Silence. No answer.

Peyton set out toward the front yard. He prayed he hadn't blown his opportunity to spend a lifetime with Erika. His stupid reaction when she told him she'd bought the ranch still echoed in his memory. Hadn't she forgiven him?

In the waning light, he spotted her leaning up against a giant oak in the front yard. She dabbed her eyes. This was more about Sandra, he figured.

He closed the gap between them, glided his hands along her arms, and coaxed her around to face him. "I'm so sorry I haven't reassured you. Sandra is gone now. I've moved on, and God has brought me face-to-face with a beautiful, godly woman. You."

"What if you can't forget about her?" She met his gaze straight on. "I can't compete with the past."

"You will never have to. Sandra is in her eternal home now. You're alive on this earth, a gift the Lord has given me. I want to marry you, Erika." He gathered her into his arms. What more could he say? "Please say yes."

"I believe you now." She whispered in his ear. "Yes, I want to be your wife."

Once again, he kneeled in front of her and pulled out the marquee diamond from the little case. After placing the ring on her left finger, he rose to brush his lips over hers then drew her closer. Her silky hair caressed his cheek, begging him to linger in their embrace.

Later, they slipped into the Adirondack chairs, his hand holding hers. The evening breeze cooled his cheeks. "As far as I'm concerned, I'd like to get married as soon as possible. The sooner we do, the sooner we can begin getting the boys' ranch up and running." He winked at her. "And the sooner we can start working on having little Peytons and Erikas. I think our families would like that."

Erika laughed. "Which do you want first, a boy or a girl?"

"Whichever God gives us." A child with Erika would never replace his baby that went to heaven with its mother, but he thanked God for a second chance at love and a family. He held her hand close to his heart. "How about you?"

"I'm ready for either." And then she sat up straight. "Peyton, there's something we need to discuss before we go any further with our plans."

Erika raised her left hand and gazed at the exquisite diamond on her finger. "Something I need to say."

Peyton peered at her, a question in his eyes.

"I should've made this clearer, but I still have obligations to my father and our family ranch."

"I understand."

"I've assured my dad that when he wants to retire, I plan to run the Ford ranch. Jace has made clear he wants to own a ranch of his own, and I don't believe Austin wants the responsibility right now."

Peyton folded his hands on his lap. "What about

your brother, the doctor?"

"I doubt that he will want to give up his practice and become a rancher. I could be wrong, but time will tell."

"So, you're saying that when the time comes, you'll need to move from the boys' home to the ranch again."

"Yes, unless the Lord intervenes. Is that a problem for us?"

Peyton leaned nearer and grasped her left hand. He lowered his lips and kissed her knuckles. "I understand perfectly. The Lord is not unaware of these things and will guide us."

"I love you, Peyton Langston."

"And I you." He paused a moment and then caught her gaze. "We can move into the house, but we won't be ready to open our doors for quite a while. I'm guessing six months to a year. There's a lot of red tape in opening a group home."

"I'm sure. Applying for a license, arranging funding, insurance matters."

"Yep, we'll have our hands full for a while."

Erika leaned to place a kiss on his delicious lips. "We can do anything as long as we have each other and the Lord."

Chapter Thirty-Six

Two months later

The autumn sun shone through the stained-glass windows at Oakville Cowboy church. Erika rested her hand on Dad's arm and glanced up at his handsome face. For the first time ever, she didn't see him through questioning eyes, wondering what he hid from her. For the first time she knew—her father loved her for who she was.

Dad smiled at her. "Erika, I am pleased to walk you down the aisle today. You're my sweet, lovely daughter, and your mother and I love you."

Dad's words lifted her like no others had, solidifying her place in his heart and their family. "November is one of my favorite months because we celebrate Thanksgiving. I'm giving thanks for you today, Dad. I love you, too."

The sight of Chet in the last row petting Sam with one hand and holding the dog's leash with the other evoked a giggle from her lips. At first when Chet asked if Sam could come to the wedding, she didn't like the idea. But now, Sam lay quietly at Chet's feet, a black and white tuxedo bow around his neck. As if he understood the gravity of the moment, he let out a long doggie sigh.

The worship leader played hers and Peyton's chosen love song on his guitar, the mellow tones signaling it was time—time to begin the trek down the long aisle past a sea of Stetsons and styled hairdos—to the altar, time for a new life as the wife of Peyton Langley.

With every step, Erika and Dad neared the front of the church and the cross mounted on a cedar wall. Three men and one lady stood on the carpeted stage. The pastor, in a western suit with a string tie and a Bible in his hand, waited. Next to him, Peyton clasped his hands in front of him and then unclasped them. His short brown hair was slicked down close to his head, and he wore a dark blue sports coat with jeans and cowboy boots. To his left, Jace, also dressed in a dark blue jacket, smiled a huge grin.

On the other side of the pastor, Charlotte, in her red velvet dress, beamed. In moments she'd perform her maid-of-honor duties and hold Erika's bouquet.

Erika savored the aroma of the fresh chrysanthemums and lilies which adorned the altar. A bridal arrangement of lavender emitted its delicate, sweet smell around her.

Finally, as she arrived at Peyton's side, Dad kissed her cheek and turned to sit with Mom in the third row.

Erika lifted her gaze to her handsome husband-to-be, his gorgeous coffee and cream eyes twinkling. Was his heart thundering in his chest as hers was?

Erika repeated her vows before the pastor, congregation and God. *Thank You, Lord, for Your grace in my life.* He'd sent her Peyton to help show her the Way. God loved her and would be with them as they lived their lives serving Him.

When the pastor finally said those words she'd longed to hear, "I pronounce you husband and wife," peace encompassed her heart. Peyton lifted a strand of her hair from her cheek and his lips met hers. Their first kiss as husband and wife.

Peyton's heart pounded at the sight of the beautiful woman floating down the aisle in a white dress. The long-sleeved lace top fit her womanly shape, and folds of some kind of white fabric flowed to the floor.

For a brief moment, the memory of another woman in a white dress pressed on his mind. He'd given his heart to her and promised to love her for as long as they both lived. But she hadn't lived—at least not on this earth. She dwelled with God now.

Though memories of Sandra would always be with him, God had blessed him with another companion. One who shared his heart to serve troubled and homeless boys.

When finally his lips met hers, peace settled in his heart. His life was complete now and he and Erika would walk together on their adventure into the future.

Erika had never seen the ranch's living and dining rooms look so festive. The catering service lived up to their promise to load the serving table with trays of cheeses and deviled eggs, baked brie bites, a pumpkin cheese ball, cranberry meatballs, and slices of pumpkin and pecan pie and cookies.

Peyton slipped his arm around her waist and nuzzled her ear. "Erika, remembering you're my wife has got my heart racing."

"You put a smile on my face every time I look at you." She held her breath, not knowing if her heart would pound out of her chest. "I love you, Peyton Langston."

Mac arrived and slapped Peyton on the back. "I always knew you two were meant for each other." Mischief danced in his eyes, as if he knew a secret.

Peyton pumped his hand. "So, you're an expert on romance these days."

Mac threw his head back in a howl. "I don't think you need any help from me, my man." He took a couple of steps back. "Congratulations, you two."

Charlotte and Jace, hand in hand, headed toward her. "We're happy for you both." Charlotte's fitted bridesmaid dress showed off her new figure.

"I can't thank you enough for helping me get started on my weight loss plan." Charotte gave a little twirl around.

Erika reached to hug her sister-in-law. "You look absolutely gorgeous. Your new shape is perfect."

Charlotte took a step closer and whispered in her ear. "Not for long. Mom and Dad Ford are going to be grandparents in another seven months. But I'm determined to get my shape back again."

Erika squealed. "Congratulations."

"Thank you both for standing up with us," Peyton said.

"We can get together any time, you know." Erika laughed. "We'll be your neighbor."

"Morning coffee or afternoon tea?" Charlotte said.

Mr. Langston approached. "I'm sorry Peyton's sister couldn't be here. She's on a mission trip to Ireland, but she sent her love and congratulations."

How different would Erika's life have been if Peyton had also served in Ireland? No, she couldn't speculate that way. She gave Mr. Langston a kiss on the cheek. "Can I call you Dad?"

"Absolutely. I'm excited to be living on the ranch with you and Peyton helping to educate and give these boys a home."

Chet grasped Pete's shirt and steered him closer to them.

Pete held the end of Sam's leash. A wide grin spanned his face. "Congratulations Miss Erika. Did you know that Chet and I are getting baptized next month?"

"Yes, and I can't wait to be there." She gave each boy a hug. "I'm glad you're waiting until after Peyton and I return from our honeymoon trip."

Peyton slipped his arm around her waist again. "One we'd better get started on soon. Our hotel is waiting, and tomorrow we've got an early morning flight from Dallas to Hawaii."

Erika slapped her cheeks. She wasn't dreaming. Soon they'd relax on the white sands of Maui, soaking up the warm sun and the blue waves.

Chapter Thirty-Seven

One year later

The vision of his wife at the writing table warmed Peyton's soul.

She glanced up. "I've got the list of things we need from the feed store." She waved a paper in the air. "I've just about finished with the ranch inventory."

He kissed the back of her neck. "Efficient as ever, honey. I noticed the horse barn angels swept and mucked out the stalls and changed their water."

She laughed. "Angels, huh? You're not giving them credit for my work."

He laughed. "Horse Haven Boys' Ranch couldn't do without you."

Apron tied around her waist, Erika stood to stir a commercial-sized pot of beef and vegetable stew in their large, open kitchen.

He neared her from behind and slipped his arms around her middle. "How's our baby today—and his or her mama?"

God had blessed him with a new family. Not only Chet and Pete and the other boys, but his father, Erika, and a new life on the way—all under one roof.

She set the spoon on the holder atop the stove and swirled in his arms to face him. "Our baby's mom is a bit nauseated these days. The doc said not to worry about it. It's to be expected for two months along."

"Did he say when you needed to stop riding Paint?"

"Yes, about twelve weeks, so you'll have to herd the sheep and ride the fence lines for me."

"Hey Peyton, you want me to check on Pete, Taylor, and Wyatt when the school bus drops them off?" Chet walked into the kitchen from the rec room. "Tell them to get started on their homework? I'm done with my online classes for today."

Peyton grinned at Chet. "Yes. And if anyone needs help with homework, you're the man since you finished your GED. How are your college classes going?"

Chet scratched the back of his neck. "I'm proud of myself, Peyton. If I put my mind to it, I can graduate university in three more years. I can't thank Mr. Ford enough for his scholarship to Texas Tech."

"Don't forget Grandpa Langston is here anytime you need help. If I'm not showing the kids how to inspect the ranch machinery or cleaning out stalls, I'm available." He slapped Chet on the shoulder. "I'm proud of you, buddy."

"Awe, thanks." Chet, two red spots on his cheeks, left by the kitchen door toward the backyard.

Peyton glanced at Erika again. "Is your job as cook extraordinaire tiring you? Dad can help out more if you need him to."

Erika shook her head. "Right now, he's getting ready to give the boys their class in caring for a horse. He wants to provide the guys some hands-on experience. Then afterward, he's picking weeds in the garden. Your father's pretty busy for the day."

"You're right about that."

"Don't forget. Jace and Charlotte will be here for dinner after a while and to play cards. Good thing my mom offered to babysit. She's ecstatic about having a granddaughter."

"And now she's going to have another grandbaby before we know it."

"We need to make the announcement to your folks soon." Erika laughed.

"You bet." Peyton paused and stared out the window of the sink. "I'm glad we're friends with Charlotte and Jace now. Your brother and I had our difficulties when I first arrived at the ranch, but now we couldn't ask for better friends."

Erika turned to him and wrapped her arms around him. "I couldn't ask for a better life."

Peyton caught her gaze and held it. "For a while, I felt as if I wandered in a desert, not sure what my purpose was. When I arrived at the Ford ranch, one of the jobs your dad assigned me was caring for flocks of sheep—like a shepherd. For once I began to feel grounded. Now, God has assigned me—and you, another shepherd's job—to take care of homeless boys." He kissed her lips. "And I haven't had a nightmare in over six months."

He turned toward his office to go over two new applications that social services sent over—a couple of boys from west Texas

Outside, one of Sam's puppies gave a friendly bark, announcing their resident boys' arrival.

Peyton relaxed at his desk and flipped open his Bible. A verse resonated in his mind, the same verse the pastor had read last Sunday. "I will repay you for the years the locusts have eaten." He flipped his Bible to Joel and read the verse out loud. God had restored his life to him.

The End

About the Author

June Foster is an award-winning author who began her writing career in an RV roaming around the USA with her husband, Joe. She brags about visiting a location before it becomes the setting in her next contemporary romance or romantic suspense. June's characters find themselves in precarious circumstances where only God can offer redemption and ultimately freedom. To date June has seen publication of over 35 novels and several devotionals.

A reader says of her debut novel Flawless: June Foster is a unique author. She has a way of looking at people and seeing what's on the inside and not what's on the outside. She loves to bring characters with unique personalities and problems to the written page.

Find June Foster at junefoster.com.

Dear Reader,

Writing *The Novice Rancher* was a sentimental journey. When I was two years old, my mother and father left California and moved to the sheep ranch which had been in my father's family for several generations. I lived the ranching life until my parents divorced when I was six. My father went on to run the ranch until he retired.

I have vague memories of those times: playing in the front yard with my cousins, exploring the bunkhouse which was empty at that time, and learning how to ride a horse.

For many years, my father sold his wool to the local coop in Sanderson, Texas where the ranch was located. Later, I remember him saying the sale of wool was no longer profitable as he couldn't beat the prices of overseas markets.

In later years, I became reacquainted with my father when I visited the ranch. I climbed the hills and descended into the canyons so prevalent in southwest Texas. I also met a couple of siblings I had never known existed until then.

Thank you, dear readers, for taking the time to read my book. I pray you enjoyed the Ford Family ranch book 1. Look for book 2, Austin's story, coming next year.

If you enjoyed The Novice Rancher, check out some of June's other titles.
The Woodlyn Series
Flawless
Out of Control
All Things New

The Almond Tree Series
For All Eternity
Echoes From the Past
What God Knew
Almond Street Mission

Small Town Romance
Letting Go
Prescription for Romance
A Harvest of Blessings
The Long Way Home

The Cranberry Cove Series
The Inn at Cranberry Cove
Love Found at Cranberry Cove
Christmas at Cranberry Cove
A Home in Cranberry Cove
Danger in Cranberry Cove

Christmas Novellas
Christmas at Raccoon Creek
A Christmas Kiss
A Kiss Under the Mistletoe

Devotional
Dancing in a Field of Daisies

Short Stories
Someone to Call His Own
An Accidental Kiss

Stand Alone Titles
Red and the Wolf
Misty Hollow
Lavender Fields Inn
Restoration of the Heart
A Home for Fritz
Dreams Deferred
An Unexpected Family
Ryan's Father
Eliza's Hope

About the bestselling Cranberry Cove series.

The Inn at Cranberry Cove – first place 2021 Selah winner in romantic suspense— Blue Ridge Mountain Christian Conference
Ashton Price arrives in Cranberry Cove, Washington, her pride wounded by her former boss. James Atwood endures punishing guilt after the death of his wife and son. Together, they must discover the mystery that haunts the Inn at Cranberry Cove. **The Inn at Cranberry Cove**

Book two continues the story: *Love Found at Cranberry Cove*
Gracie Mayberry wants to study marine science at the community college in a neighboring coastal town. Seattle resident Blake Sloan admits he's followed his father's dream instead of his heart's desire—to run his own business and start a non-profit to benefit wounded vets. But when a stalker makes terrifying midnight visits to the humble Mayberry home and threatens their lives, Blake discovers he's also a target of extortion. Can Blake and Gracie learn who's behind the danger that threatens them? Will a small-town girl and big-city boy find a life together? **Love Found at Cranberry Cove**

In Book three: *Christmas at Cranberry*

Cove

Ryder Langston retires from commercial fishing and manages Blake Sloan's supply stores. When the owner of the inn in Cranberry Cove hires a new executive chef, Ryder is intrigued by the tall woman with ebony hair who hides a dark family secret.

Juliette Duplay must flee from her French roots and her past when a family member turns against her. She'd like to blend into the American culture but can't escape danger even in the small community of Cranberry Cove.

Can Ryder and Juliette unravel the mystery in time to celebrate *Christmas at Cranberry Cove?* **Christmas at Cranberry Cove**

In Book four, Madison and Micah run from their past. *A Home in Cranberry Cove*

Madison Mitchell will never trust a man again. The love of her life broke her heart and married a French chef. Now she throws herself into her work at The Inn at Cranberry Cove. When she accidentally tangles with the manager of a nearby fishing supply store, she suspects the handsome guy is hiding something.

Micah Collins flees Sacramento seeking solace in the seaside village in Washington state. But he discovers an enemy has followed him to Cranberry Cove. He must endure frightful threats at the same time keeping his previous life secret. When Madison finds herself in danger, Micah blames himself.

Madison and Micah are haunted by someone from Micah's past, but is the culprit the real enemy or should they look elsewhere? Will they find a future together?

A Home in Cranberry Cove

Book Five *Danger in Cranberry Cove* **Julie and Lucas discover a 15-year-old secret.**
When Julie Wilder joins local lawyer Lucas Ethridge in uncovering clues of who murdered their high school friend on the beach fifteen years before, anonymous phone calls from someone who claims to be the killer are unnerving. After incriminating evidence turns up, can Lucas and Julie discover the killer's identity or will they suffer the same fate as their friend? **Danger in Cranberry Cove**